Little Birds

and Other Small Magic

Small Magic Series
Book 1

Sarah Buckleitner

EBook ISBN: 979-8-9895491-0-8
Trade Paperback ISBN: 979-8-9895491-1-5
Hardcover ISBN: 979-8-9895491-2-2

Author: Sarah R Buckleitner
Cover Design: S.D. Youngmann
Editor: Ann Marie Hormeku

Published by SkyShark Publishers
PO Box 39
Colbert, GA 30628
Ann Marie Hormeku, Publisher
SkyShark Publishers Edition 2023

Printed in the USA

Join our SkyShark Readers Group for new projects, and giveaways. Sign up at www.SkySharkPub.com

For my mom, for teaching me about the highest highs and lowest lows of love. And my real-life-Theo. Thanks for being my warm hand to hold through it all.

Chapter One

MARY ELOISE MOORE ELLMIRE opened her bedroom window for the first time in her life on her eighteenth birthday. It wasn't easy—many years and wet seasons had swollen the wood. It groaned as she pressed, but finally its grip loosened. A chill spring breeze reached in to ruffle her hair—Mary frowned, and patted the mussed locks quickly back into place.

The open window was an invitation. Not for a lover. Mary would have died at the mere thought of a man climbing into her bedroom. But for a bird. A small bird, white as the first snowfall in November, with shiny black eyes. Perhaps most notably, it'd be carrying a scroll.

Mary pushed her glasses up on her nose and glanced sharply into the trees. But no—it was only a seagull breaking free from the pines and wheeling back toward the sea. Her straight little back shivered with the brief excitement of it.

Your bird would find you on your eighteenth birthday whether your window was open or not. Tommy Edelstein's had even found him while he was in the outhouse—it had squeezed in through the carved half-moon in the door and dropped its scroll in his lap. He'd had to scramble to catch it before it fluttered down into the abyss.

The story about Tommy Edelstein had struck Mary with particular horror. Imagine you lost your scroll before you could read it! What would you do, with no destiny to guide you?

Because that was what was on the scroll—your destiny.

She had resolved to take no risks. She would receive her destiny as sensibly as she did everything else, waiting for it by the open window.

Downstairs, she heard the first creaks of the day. Her father must be awake now, and getting the fire going again. It was still chilly, especially in the lower parts of the house, where the sun wouldn't shine in for some time.

On any other day she'd hurry downstairs to help—she'd stir the scrambled eggs while her father stoked the fire. And then her mother would escort her to the church, where she'd sit in one of the hard, wooden pews and spend an hour praying prior to Bible study with Augustus Primrose, the preacher's third son.

Today, she waited until she heard the clatter of silverware on the table before she padded down the stairs in her stockinged feet. Surely, she thought, a scroll couldn't get lost at the breakfast table.

All other matters would have to wait until tomorrow, when her destiny was tacked securely to the wooden plaque waiting on the living room wall downstairs.

Her parents' scrolls already hung above that plaque, their paper yellowed with age. As she sat down at the breakfast table, she peered through the fragrant steam of the thick slabs of bacon sizzling on the woodstove, and read the familiar, slanted writing.

Her mother's read: Fight your facial hair preferences

when choosing a man! True love lies beneath hair. It was one of the rare destinies that didn't mention a career, and so her mother had married her father—who had a great, bushy mustache, just like his father, and funneled her energies into raising Mary.

Her father's destiny had been much more straightforward: Carry the mail and marry Eloise Moore! He was younger than her mother—poor Eloise had spent a confused few months wondering which hairy man she ought to marry until Bradley had turned eighteen and cleared it up.

Mary hoped that her destiny was more like her father's than her mother's. In fact, she had some idea of what she might like it to say, even though she'd tried very hard not to hope for one particular thing.

When she glanced at her hopes out of the corner of her eye, it was clear that she hoped it would tell her to be a seamstress, and marry Augustus Primrose. Mary had had to try very hard not to notice the way a single auburn curl slipped down his forehead as he bent over his bible this last year.

On the table, a jug of frothy, still-warm milk waited in the white-porcelain pitcher. Her mother had baked iced sugar cookies for her yesterday and frosted them in the shapes of little white birds with scrolls, along with the traditional birthday fairies and flowers.

Privately, Mary thought that they were a bit childish for an eighteenth birthday, but she would never dare say so to her mother.

"Happy birthday!" her father boomed at her, turning from the stove. He bristled her cheek with his snowy white mustache.

"Happy birthday!" her mother trilled, the thin lips Mary had inherited turned up to beaming. "No birdies yet?"

"None yet," said Mary. Her voice came out brittle,

betraying her disappointment that her destiny hadn't cooperated by fluttering in the window first thing that morning.

"Ah well, mine didn't arrive until an hour before dusk," her father told her as he scooped the bacon onto a plate and set it next to the platter of eggs. They smiled sunnily at her from the table. "Ellmires have always been afternooners."

The front door rattled, and then burst open.

Everyone at the table jumped, but it was only Mary's best friend, Delia, her face framed by a cloud of black hair. Her shirt was singed at the hem, and Mary could see a new burn—red and angry against the deep brown of her wrist, likely from an early shift with the blacksmith. Delia wasn't eighteen yet, but she was one of those who liked to tempt fate by tinkering in love and careers.

"Morning, Ellmires!" she said. "And happy birthday to you, dear friend! Did it come? Are you soon to be Mrs. Primrose?"

Mary choked on her milk.

Mary's dad thwacked her on the back. "I hope you mean Augustus Primrose. If the other Primrose boys aren't fit for the cloth, they certainly aren't fit for my little girl's hand. Especially that Theodore. Mrs. Dennison says he shot his dog's leg clean off in a fit of rage! Can you imagine?!"

Mary's mother's lips practically disappeared as she imagined.

"I've heard it too," said Delia, grabbing a second cookie with a decided nod. "I can't blame Pastor Primrose for promising the rectory to Augustus. The way Theodore is always tromping around in the woods like some sort of wild man—"

"And that beard—" exclaimed Mary's mother.

"Just think, if your bird were to have you marry someone like that," said Delia, black eyes dancing.

"There is no bird yet," Mary repeated, voice quivery. She'd gone very pale. Her digestion wasn't good at the best of times and now her appetite seemed to have disappeared altogether.

"Have a cookie, dear," her mother said, and pushed the plate toward Mary. "You know, my bird came just as I'd risen from bed. I was caught fully off guard—imagine getting your destiny in your dressing gown!" She smiled warmly at Mary, who had been fully dressed since before the sun had risen to prevent that exact occurrence.

Mary took a cookie—a white bird—and bit off a wing. Her mother's iced cookies were famous for how the icing melted like spun sugar on your tongue—but Mary could hardly swallow. Her stomach twisted with nerves.

"May I be excused?" she asked after she had choked it down with several long draughts of sweet spring milk.

"Of course!" said her mother.

"Would you like me to wait with you?" asked Delia, spearing a slab of bacon on her fork.

"That's very kind of you, but I think I'd best wait alone." They all watched as the back of her head—her thin hair in a limp braid—disappeared up the stairs.

"What a strange child we've produced," her father said. He grabbed the largest sugar cookie—a male fairy grinning cheekily at them from behind a toadstool.

"As long as she doesn't become as odd as your mother," said Mary's mother delicately as she delivered a plate loaded with eggs and bacon to Delia.

He laughed aloud at that. "She'd have to fall right off the opposite side of the wagon. Well, Delia, how's your family?"

Upstairs, in the bedroom above the stairwell, Mary perched in her window seat and listened as the bells counted off yet another hour. Below, the thicket of trees only grew stiller with the warming day.

She wasn't sure where to look—at the pines at the base of the mountain? At the cluster of apple trees away across town, with the lake gleaming at their feet? At the bell tower that Tolling Bell had been named for, tucked between lofty oaks?

No one knew where the little white birds with their fate-telling scrolls came from. They had been coming since the beginning of time and were as much a part of life in the little Maine village as snowfall in winter or losing your baby teeth.

At two hours past breakfast, a flock of seagulls flew low over the roof of the house, and she startled so badly that she nearly fell out the window.

At three hours past, she developed a headache from staring at the oaks through her funny round glasses—which were intended solely for stitching, and not general wear—and still, no bird had emerged.

Around supper time her father came upstairs with a ham sandwich wrapped in a blue checked napkin, a mug of milk, and a tower of sugar cookies. "Maybe you ought to take a break," he said kindly. "Pick up some stitching, have a cookie. The bird will come whether you're watching for it or not."

Her stomach had only grown worse since breakfast, but she did take up her latest piece of needlepoint—an intricate rose pattern for one of the parlor pillows downstairs. The work kept her mind off the woods, but when a cardinal fluttered onto one of the spindly branches of the apple tree below her window, she jabbed herself so hard with her needle that she was forced to get up and find a napkin to blot the wound.

There was no bird waiting for her when she returned. Nor was there one when she came back up after dinner—

which was a shepherd's pie loaded with savory chunks of beef and studded with peas. It was her favorite meal, but tonight she could hardly swallow a bite.

The air was growing cooler now, and the light rapidly dimmer. Mary could feel her heart pick up tempo in her chest. No bird had ever come after dark—surely it must arrive any minute now.

But the more she watched, the less likely it seemed to ever come.

As the bells tolled 8 p.m., Mary imagined that they had a sorrowful tone to them. And then the sun slipped away behind the mountains on the other side of the valley, and a slim sickle moon rose up behind the pine stand.

Mary sat in stunned stillness at the window. The day was over, and still no bird had come.

Chapter Two

WHEN IT WAS WELL and truly dark, there was a knock on her door.

"Come in," she said, voice tremulous.

The door burst open. "Well?" her mother asked, beaming. Her father was peering out from behind her mother's bony frame, his hair shining silver in the candlelight. He too was grinning, though rather forcibly, as though he were determined to smile no matter what Mary's destiny read.

"It—it hasn't—" Mary's voice sputtered out into silent tears.

Her parents crossed the room in two large bounds.

"Hasn't come!"

"What ever do you mean?"

"Surely it must have come—"

Mary shook her head tearfully. "It hasn't, I'm quite sure. I haven't moved from the window all afternoon."

That was clear from her unusually rumpled dress, and her pale, drawn face. Her mother bustled off immediately to make tea—Moores always make tea in times of crisis—and her father guided her to the bed with one firm hand.

"We'll get this all sorted," he said as he blotted her tears with her needlework. Mary didn't ask what he meant—she knew it was empty comfort. There was nothing to sort. There was no one to complain to, no one to inquire of. You can't ask the stars and the trees why a destiny didn't arrive when it should've.

Her mother brought up peppermint tea laced with honey and insisted that Mary sip it to soothe her stomach and nerves. She did as she was told, and then allowed them to put her to bed and blow out the candle.

But the white light of the moon shone in through the window and kept her awake, taunting her, whispering that it had risen and her little white bird still hadn't arrived.

What was a person without a destiny to do? She'd have no career. No great loves or great friendships. Nothing whatsoever to live for. Worse, she'd be different now. Marked forever as the girl who didn't have a destiny.

As far as she knew, no one in the entire history of Tolling Bell had ever not received a destiny. Why her, why now? Perhaps it would be best to die right off. A little sob escaped her throat at this, and she thought with sad satisfaction that no one would really miss her, except perhaps her parents—and what did they count?

She felt keenly the loss of all the things that she had hoped for—the tidy brick rectory, Augustus Primrose reading verses aloud to her from a black book of morals, trimming her new curtains with needlework tulips. Apprenticing with formidable Mr. Button, the town tailor, and learning to trim hats and craft fashions that all the town's ladies donned. Bringing home a fat, sweet baby to snuggle and rock and tuck into bed.

At that thought, a small wail escaped from her mouth, and

a fresh wave of tears came sailing down her cheeks with the silent dignity that comes from deep self-pity.

When at last she slept, she dreamt morbid dreams of the townspeople filing out of the pines on the hill to stand under her window and jeer at her. Each had a small white bird perched on their shoulder, and they glared at her out of those shiny black eyes until she felt her own eyes prickle with the injustice of it all.

She woke suddenly, just as the bells tolled two in the morning. It had just occurred to her, as if her mind had been turning all the while she'd been asleep, that perhaps it wasn't that her bird hadn't come, but that her parents had gotten her birth date wrong! Hope flared in her chest like a bonfire.

She jumped up at once and, shivering in her thin cotton nightgown, tiptoed downstairs to the great oak desk where her parents kept their important documents. Her hands shook as she lit a candle.

It took a few long moments of sorting through papers, some so fragile that she feared they'd crumble at her touch, their ink so faint that she had to hold them right up to the candle to read their headings, before she found her birth certificate.

It was plain and sturdy, like all of the birth certificates in Tolling Bell. And there was her birthdate, plainly stamped below her name.

MARY ELOISE MOORE ELLMIRE
Born **APRIL 16TH, 1897** at **11:14 AM**
to *BRADLEY CHARLES ELLMIRE*
and *ELOISE MOORE ELLMIRE*
TOWN AND DISTRICT OF TOLLING BELL, MAINE

Mary felt her heart sink. It was all correct. Yesterday had

been the sixteenth of April, and already now it was the seventeenth. Her eighteenth birthday had come and gone without a destiny.

She gathered the documents with shaky hands and placed them in their bundle in the third drawer of the desk. Hopeless again, she crept back upstairs, and stared into the indeterminate darkness above her bed until dawn.

In the morning, after the church bell had tolled and Mary still hadn't emerged from her room, her parents held a hushed conference outside of her silent door.

"Have you ever heard of anyone not receiving their destiny before?" Her mother's face was drawn with worry.

"It's unheard of," her father whispered back.

"I just don't understand. Why our Mary? She's such a good girl."

He shook his head sadly. "I don't know, Eloise. Everyone gets a destiny—everyone. Even that terrible Primrose boy. I'm fully certain it has nothing to do with goodness."

"What do we do?"

"We'll leave her alone," her father decided, "until she feels ready to face it."

So leave her alone they did, though her mother delivered what she hoped would be a heartening porridge, laced with cream and brown sugar sprinkled in the shape of a smiley face. She left it at the foot of the door with a knock and a cheery, "There's breakfast at the door, if you want it!"

Mary did not respond, and at lunch the bowl of porridge was back outside the door with only a single bite taken from it, the smile intact but melted into a sort of grimace from the heat. A child with more spirit might have at least turned the smile into a frown, reflected her mother as she carried it downstairs to offer to her husband. That seemed infinitely preferable to this suffering silence.

It didn't take long for word of Mary's misery to leak out. Mrs. Ellmire told Mrs. Dennison as she went to fetch the morning's milk, and Mr. Dennison overheard, and told his eldest son—who had turned eighteen two months before, and had received the lackluster destiny of distributing the bi-monthly town newsletter and living with his parents.

And he of course told everyone with a vengeance, for any destiny is better than no destiny at all, and it made them forget their own pity for him.

Mary's cousins, the Moores, took special affront to her lack of destiny. They had been one of the first families in Tolling Bell, and were known for their moral fortitude and strength of character. Everyone had always said that Mary was much more a Moore than an Ellmire, and now the association shamed them.

"She is half Ellmire," they reminded everyone who brought it up to them. "You know how that goes."

Soon the whole town of Tolling Bell was buzzing with the news of poor destinyless Mary Ellmire, locked up all alone in her room.

A WEEK CAME AND WENT, and still Mary hadn't come down from her room. Her parents brought her meals three times a day, which she picked at before sending back down. In between, she sprawled across her bed—which was still tidily made—in hopeless silence, the deepening circles under her eyes a reflection of her woes.

Her tears had dried up since that first night. Instead, her grief permeated the house in the form of bottomless silence. Even the house itself quieted in the face of her pain—the logs burned with nary a snap or pop, and the stairs hardly creaked, even under her father's bulk.

A series of visitors trooped steadily through the house, though they seemed to only deepen the silence with their somberness and pity. First was Mrs. Dennison, driven by a sense of neighborliness and a keen desire to see if a destinyless person looked any different than a regular person. Her curiosity was never filled—the Ellmires accepted the meat pie she pressed on them with gracious thanks, and then ushered her toward the door.

She did, however, catch a glimpse of the invalid through the still-open window of the room upstairs, her glasses reflecting the great expanse of overcast sky outside.

Mrs. Dennison—her own eyes being poor—mistook the glimmering white ovals as a sign that Mary had gone blind with grief, and soon a second rumor was raging through town that not only was Mary Ellmire destinyless, but that she'd lost her vision to boot.

The second visitor was Pastor Primrose, the day after Mary had missed church for the first time in her life. He knocked soberly upon the door—three hard knocks—and then insisted that he be let up to speak with Mary.

"What do you plan to say to her?" asked Mr. Ellmire, his mustache bristling defensively.

"She needs advisement to confess her sins. Surely the girl has done something to bring this upon herself." Pastor Primrose's ears went red at being questioned so impertinently.

The bellow that chased the pastor out of the house wasn't godly, but it kept Mary free from chastisement.

Finally, a figure who might actually do Mary some good appeared on the doorstep. Delia Trotter, carrying a clump of daisies.

It was with great hope that Mr. and Mrs. Ellmire ushered

her up the stairs to Mary's room, but Delia returned only ten minutes later, shaking her head dejectedly.

"I've never seen such a downtrodden little personage," she said in the tone of one delivering an expert opinion. "I couldn't get more than five words from her. She just shivered and looked out of that terrible, open window."

Another hushed meeting was held between her parents when Delia had gone, this time in the stairwell. Mrs. Ellmire clutched yet another mug of tea—this one gone stone cold after having been abandoned outside Mary's door.

"We've got to do something!" sputtered her father. "This can't go on much longer!"

"But what is there to do with her? No one will take her on as an apprentice, not without a destiny. And I can't imagine we'd find anyone to marry her. Perhaps if she were a beauty—"

But no, Mary was certainly not a beauty, not with those odd wire glasses she insisted on wearing to magnify her stitches—despite her eyesight being perfectly fine—and her thin, colorless hair. Not even with her beautiful Ellmire eyes —her lashes were too thin, her nose too narrow, her frame too wretchedly skinny.

"Do you have any relatives back in Portland who might take her...?" asked Mrs. Ellmire, with the air of one grasping at straws.

"Send our Mary to that backwards place? They're twisted there, Eloise. Twisted. They get all mixed up about how to do things without destinies to guide them—you're hanged if you look different or act different or marry someone you ought'nt. Half of them are crooks! I wouldn't send her there if it were the end of the world!" boomed Mr. Ellmire.

They both sighed. Mrs. Ellmire's chin sunk into her hand. "She can't stay here. She'll waste away up there, cross-stitching till her fingers are worn to the bone and her eyes can't see beyond her lap. She needs something to do. Something to give her purpose."

"There is one thing—" began Mr. Ellmire, with a careful glance at his wife. When she only lifted her gaze to meet his, he continued. "We could ask Grandma Isabella whether she has any ideas. She might know of other places that get destinies, and perhaps we could bring Mary there. And if not, well, she said last week at the market that she was having trouble managing on her own—perhaps Mary could stay with her? Help her out?"

Mrs. Ellmire's chin shot straight out of her hand. "Go to stay with Grandma! But she's as nutty as squirrel poo!" Her cheeks flushed immediately, as though in a silent reprimand to such vulgar language, but she didn't take it back.

"Now Eloise," Mr. Ellmire laid a heavy hand on her shoulder. "Isabella raised me, and I turned out normal as pie. She's a fine woman, and she's got enough fire in her to wake Mary up. Perhaps they'll balance each other out a bit. Mary will civilize Grandma, and Grandma will give Mary a little spunk. Plus, she needs the help. It's the Christian thing, to help a little old lady."

They looked at each other in the dark stairwell. "Well," Mrs. Ellmire said at last. "At least it's something—I'll walk over to Grandma's tomorrow to talk to her."

Mr. Ellmire sighed, his body deflating like a great balloon. For the first time since Mary's birthday, he felt slightly less helpless. It is a terrible thing to watch your beloved child suffer with no course of action to take on their behalf. He just hoped his formidable mother would know how help her—if anyone could, it was her.

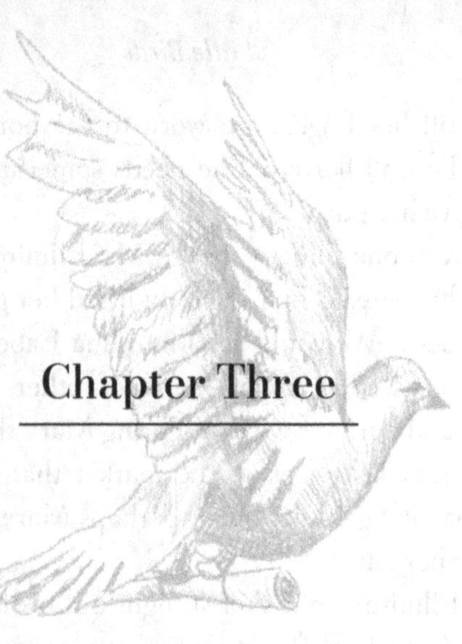

Chapter Three

IN THE MORNING—ONE of those frigid spring mornings that feels as though winter is trying to slip back onto the landscape —Mrs. Ellmire pinned on her warmest, reddest traveling cloak, and headed out across town and into the big woods on the far side of the church.

Grandma Isabella lived in the furthest reaches of what could still be called Tolling Bell. The only ones who lived further were those wild Primrose boys, though it was a different matter for young men to live so far out than it was for an elderly woman.

Mrs. Ellmire followed the mossy trail to the clearing where Isabella's cabin perched against the trees. Smoke curled out of the chimney, and the first spring buds bloomed in the garden out front. Behind the cabin, a cheerful stream burbled before it arched away into the woods again. She paused in front of the cardinal red door, hand poised to knock.

After her husband had died, Grandma Isabella had quit her position as the headmistress of the school, sold their grand, respectable townhouse, and stopped going to church. Now on Sundays, she carted a wagon full of homegrown vegetables around to all the poorest families and muttered that she was doing "real" good. Worse yet, she was known throughout the town as being a witch, because she specialized in gathering plants from the wilderness and cooking them.

Seeking her opinion was a drastic solution, and a risky one. With the town already in turmoil over Mary's lack of destiny, adding Grandma's outlandish reputation on top of it all might only fan the flames. But Grandma might have answers as to why Mary's destiny hadn't come, and whether it'd ever happened before. She'd been alive for over eight decades, and she'd often fielded questions from her pupils about the destiny-carrying birds.

Mrs. Ellmire knocked once, twice, and then the door creaked lustily open and the bright blue eye of Isabella Ellmire peered out through the crack.

"Hello deary," she said upon seeing her daughter-in-law. "Do come in, come in."

The cabin was warm and cheery—dried herbs hung from the ceiling, and knobbly blue vases held bouquets of pinecones and evergreen. A squat woodstove shimmered with heat in the corner, and a rug as red as pine needles kept the chill stone floor at bay.

It wasn't a bad setup, thought Mrs. Ellmire, though rather dustier than what she'd have in her own home.

Living so far out of town, Isabella hadn't yet heard of their predicament with Mary, and Mrs. Ellmire explained the matter as succinctly as she could. When she'd finished, silence hung in the air, punctuated only by the chirrups of the cardinals on the feeder outside the kitchen window.

"Poor Mary," said Grandma Isabella at last. She was seated at the kitchen table, and she took a thoughtful sip of her coffee before she went on. "I can't imagine the townsfolk have taken kindly to the news."

"They certainly have not," said Mrs. Ellmire sadly. "We've managed to keep most of it from Mary, but you should hear the rumors going around. Terrible things—that Mary did something so that the birds didn't find her worthy of a destiny. Others are saying it's a sign of the end times coming and that soon we won't have destinies at all. We can hardly send her out into town with folks saying things like that, it'd simply crush her!"

Grandma glowered over her coffee, and her fingers tightened on the handle of her brown speckled mug. "This town is full of complete nincompoops."

Mrs. Ellmire pursed her lips at the foul language, but she couldn't bring herself to disagree. Instead, she ran a forefinger absently over the back of one of the kitchen chairs. It came away gray with dust, and she held it away from herself as she said, "Bradley and I were wondering if you knew anything more about the destinies. Whether you'd ever heard of someone not receiving one before."

"No," said Grandma frankly. "Never, not once in my eighty-eight years. Of course, folks outside of Tolling Bell don't receive destinies, and I remember hearing once that Dennis Crimmers, who was born here, didn't receive one after he'd moved away."

"And there are no towns where people receive them later than eighteen years of age? I did think perhaps we could try to bring her somewhere else—"

"No, no," said Grandma. "Tolling Bell is the only place where I've heard of people receiving destinies. Of course, we keep it quiet, so perhaps there are other places where folks keep the magic close to their chests. And I have heard whispers of different kinds of magic—a town where each new baby is born with the soul of one of its ancestors, and another where people live longer than would usually be expected—but nothing like what we have here..."

Mrs. Ellmire sighed, her last hope slipping away with Grandma's words. "I just don't know what to do with the girl. She's seemed only half alive this last week, gazing out of her open window, chilled half to the bone. But I can't see that sending her out into the world will be any better."

"Something has to be done," agreed Grandma Isabella. "I'll take the girl, put her to work. I'm getting too old to chop wood for the stove anyhoo. It's the perfect solution—it'll give some purpose to her days, but she'll be out of the way of the townsfolk and all their opinions."

Mrs. Ellmire couldn't very well see Mary chopping wood, but it seemed a better way to pass the time than withering away in her room. "It's settled then. We'll gather her things and have her here by tomorrow evening."

They shook on it, a solid handshake between two women, and Mrs. Ellmire headed home to tell her husband the news.

AT SUPPER THE NEXT DAY, Mrs. Ellmire knocked on her daughter's door, a plate of toast slathered with currant jam and butter in one hand. But this time she didn't set the plate down and leave. When a moment elapsed without a word, she knocked again. Mr. Ellmire hovered behind her like an anxious bear.

"Come in," said a tremulous voice.

She swung the door open with some trepidation—who knew what changes the last week might have wrought in Mary. But to her great relief, despite a rumpled head of hair and dark shadows beneath her eyes, her daughter looked largely the same. It seemed that not even grief could alter constant little Mary Ellmire.

The room was the same as ever, except for the open window, which wafted chilling spring air over them all and made it colder than an icebox.

"Mary," she began, but the words stuck in her throat, and she couldn't get them out.

"Mary," boomed Mr. Ellmire, taking up the mantle. "This nonsense has gone on too long. Sure, a destiny may not have come for you. You're just going to have to buck up and make your own destiny. And you won't do it moping around this room."

It wasn't the way Mrs. Ellmire would have said it—she thought the term 'buck up' was altogether too harsh—but it did the job. "We're sending you to Grandma Isabella's. She's getting up there anyway and could use an extra hand. She said you'd be very welcome."

Any other young woman would have stamped her feet at the notion of being sent to live with a stodgy, disreputable old relative who lived in the woods. But Mary just bowed her head and helped to pack up a trunk with her things.

Her mother perched on the edge of the bed as she packed. "I know this must seem awfully harsh..." She let her voice fade out, inviting Mary's opinion. None came. "But you know, my destiny wasn't as straightforward as some. And at first I felt very lost. Even after I married your father, I wished there had been some no-nonsense line about what I should do with my time. It took many years before you were born, so I had quite a while to wish."

Mary's fingers trembled as she folded a sweater.

"It wasn't until I had you, dear, that I felt like I had a purpose—" her voice cracked. "So we're sending you to Grandma's so that you might have a purpose. She's getting older, and managing isn't as easy as it once was for her. She needs a helper, and I know you'll do the job admirably." Eloise reached out to stroke Mary's thin hair, and tears glistened in her eyes at the prospect of sending her little girl away.

After a moment, Mary lifted one chilly, frail hand, and placed it on her mother's arm comfortingly. She kept her face turned toward the window so that her mom wouldn't see the tears threatening to overflow from her own eyes.

The sun was just beginning to sink below the mountains as they set out for Grandma Isabella's, Mary bundled up in her charcoal grey cloak with the silver clasp at the throat, her father hoisting her trunk on one broad shoulder.

She kept the hood up as they walked through town, feeling the pitying gazes of the townsfolk upon her like frostbite. It was a relief to step into the trees. At least the woods didn't know that she was doomed—or if they did, they didn't pity her. No tree had ever received a destiny.

Soon they spied the cottage, tucked in among the pines like a gingerbread house in a fairytale.

The door swung open to greet them as they stomped the mud off their boots at the end of Grandma's stone walkway. The smell of baking bread wafted out like a cloud. Grandma Isabella stood in the midst of the heavenly smell, tiny and fierce eyed, her white hair flying off in every direction. But her voice was kind, and the hand she placed on Mary's bony shoulder to welcome her was gentle.

"You'll have to sleep in the loft," she said as Mr. Ellmire looked for a good space to set the trunk down. It was a thirty-minute walk to Grandma's, much of it uphill, and his daughter's accoutrements were substantial. He'd already sweated through his shirt. "I've only got the one bedroom. But it'll be cozy enough up there."

Mary followed her father and trunk up the tightly wound wooden stairs and found herself in her new bedroom. If she'd been in any other state of mind, she'd have found it pleasant—there was a fleecy lambswool rug on the floor to protect her bare feet from the cold in the mornings, and the bed was low to the ground and thick with patchwork quilts.

The top quilt had several holes, but the colors were bright and cheery, and it lent a lived-in feeling to the space that her own room lacked. On the wall opposite the bed, Grandma Isabella had hung a wreath of evergreen, and an oil lamp on her bedside table shone brightly against the growing darkness.

The bed abutted double windows, under a low alcove and pitched roof. The windows looked out over the woods to the north—Mary could just make out the sparkle of a lake through the trees, glinting pink in the sunset. A yellow light shone steadily off the bank—Mary supposed it must be from another cottage. It looked very welcoming in the dim gloom of the woods.

Something about the sight cheered her marginally, and she found she was able to hug her parents goodbye with only one or two tears—quickly swiped away from her cheeks and absorbed into her thick muslin gown. Her parents didn't fare quite as well: her mother's shoulders shook and Mr. Ellmire sniffled into his mustache. They looked very forlorn as they walked down the trail alone together, back to town.

Mary's heart ached for them, all alone now in their big house, and for herself, stuck out here with the town reprobate. But she squared her shoulders and turned to Grandma. This was her life now—she might as well face it full on.

Grandma opened her mouth to speak—for a moment Mary feared that she was about to comment on the fact that she had no destiny, and she braced herself. But all Grandma said was, "I was planning on rabbit stew for dinner, and I've got a loaf just about ready to come out of the oven. Perhaps you could cut the carrots."

Mary nodded with relief and followed her inside to help prepare dinner. They ate at the small silvery oak table, and forced by the call of duty to be a polite house guest, she was able to eat first one bite, and then another, until finally the bowl was clean.

She may not have gone back for seconds like Grandma Isabella, but it was the most food she'd eaten in a week, and she felt stronger for it. They washed up in silence, Mary scrubbing the earthenware bowls while Grandma Isabella dried and stacked them on the wooden shelf that held her pottery.

When the kitchen was tidy again, Grandma retired to her bedroom. She wasn't the sort to hover, a fact for which Mary was grateful. She ascended the spiral staircase to her bedroom and sat on the bed for a long minute fully dressed, looking out over the darkened trees and the spangle of stars in the sky. She wondered whether all the rest of her life would be spent chopping carrots in Grandma Isabella's kitchen.

It was better than any alternative that she could see. Still, she ached for the simple life she had left behind. When her destiny had failed to come, she'd lost not only her future, but her present life, too.

She missed her bedroom, with its intricately embroidered curtains and tidy, narrow bed, and early mornings cooking alongside her father, and the familiar smell of her mother's hair. At the thought of her mother, the tears she'd suppressed all day slipped silently down her cheeks and into the shabby patchwork quilt.

THE NEXT MORNING Grandma Isabella woke her early with a shout up the stairs. The forest outside the window was still dark, and the birds filled the trees with their raucous early morning song. "Dress in the most sensible thing you own," she instructed through the floorboards. "We have a big day ahead of us."

By the time Mary had dressed—in her stiffest grey muslin —and made her way downstairs, a black kettle of coffee burbled and eggs with deep orange yolks sizzled on the stove.

Mary had never tasted coffee before, and she nearly spat it out with her first sip, but Grandma showed her how to sweeten it with honey and fresh cream (hiding her smile very neatly with a duck behind the cream jug), and then it went down much more smoothly.

It was a simple breakfast—just the eggs and leftover bread from the day before—but Mary could only nibble at it. She was nervous about the day ahead, and her stomach had tightened accordingly. Grandma eyed the leftovers disdainfully, but then took care of the matter by wolfing them down herself, along with the rest of the coffee.

"I can't abide food waste," she told Mary when the girl eyed her with something a bit like fear. "We'll make sure you're hungry for supper."

Mary nodded to be agreeable, though she couldn't see why it mattered whether she was hungry or not. Mary was not the type to break rules, and now that she knew it was a house rule not to waste food, she'd make herself sick before she left food on her plate again.

Outside, the day was dawning cool and fine. A crust of frost coated the grass, and melting dew drops shimmered rainbow in the sunshine.

They started at the wood pile. "Better to get this chore over with early, while it's still cool," Grandma said. "And take those ridiculous glasses off. They'll throw off your aim." Mary took off the glasses and slipped them into her pocket with care. It felt an awfully harsh blow to have to remove them—the world was too sharp and too bright.

She squinted against the early morning sun, which glared through the trees like it had a personal vendetta against her. Grandma Isabella demonstrated how to hold and swing the axe.

"You'll want your hands here and here," she said, handing the axe over and briskly sliding Mary's delicate fingers over the rough wood.

The axe felt very heavy and awkward in her arms. She gave it an experimental swing toward the piece of wood Grandma had lined up on the stump and missed entirely.

"No, no, no," chided Grandma Isabella. "Put your feet here and here, like this. And you'll want to get a good swing up so that the weight of the axe helps with the work."

Mary positioned her feet in the stiff leather boots that chafed so uncomfortably against her skin and raised the axe again. This time it hit the log, but merely glanced off, taking a small chip with it.

"You're doing it all wrong," said Grandma, rather sharpish. "You've got to put your back into it!"

"I'm trying! Can't you see that I'm trying!" shouted Mary suddenly, flinging the axe into the grass.

The outburst startled them both. Mary had never lost her temper that way before—never had spoken back to an elder. Her eyes grew very wide, and her face got very white, and she turned to Grandma with an apology ready to tumble from her lips.

But, to her surprise, Grandma was smiling—a great, gap-toothed smile, much broader than the sly smirk she'd hid behind the cream jug during breakfast. "That's more like it. Takes a bit of spirit to chop wood. Now try again."

She held the offending axe out like a peace offering.

Mary took it, swung the axe high up above her head and channeled her rage against Grandma and the unfairness of life into one mighty chop. With a satisfying thwunk the log split along the grain into two tidy pieces. Grandma caught them and tossed them easily into the wood bin.

She nodded in stern approval, a smile twitching on her lips. Mary frowned back at her, even though it had been satisfying splitting the wood so easily in two.

While she shook out her arms and got back into her stance, Grandma set another log on the stump. Thwunk went the axe. This time Mary couldn't help it—her face cracked into a smile.

Chapter Four

THEY CHOPPED WOOD ALL MORNING, until wood halves littered the yard, and Grandma instructed her to gather them up and carry them inside, where they were to be arranged in a tidy pile next to the woodstove. As Mary stepped back to look at the little pyramid she'd created, she felt the same swelling pride that she did when she finished a sewing project—though her arms were significantly more tired.

Then it was back outside, this time to the large garden that Grandma kept around the rear of the house, uphill from where the stream rounded in its horseshoe before heading north again, through the woods to the lake.

Grandma's garden was famous throughout Tolling Bell. Her squash grew the biggest, her pumpkins the orange-est, her tomatoes the shiniest and sweetest.

It was too early in the season for any leafy heads to poke above the soil, but the fence had been torn in places during the winter and had to be mended to keep the deer and rabbits at bay. Wildlife abounded in the deep woods surrounding the cabin and according to Grandma, they loved nothing more than a bite of homegrown produce for supper.

Grandma showed her how to twist the wire fencing together to mend holes, and how to hammer the wooden stakes that held it up deeper into the loamy earth. It was painstaking work, but it kept Mary's mind off of her woes, and so she threw her back into it and didn't complain.

It helped that hammering and twisting came more naturally to Mary than chopping, because Grandma Isabella kept her criticisms to herself, and twisted away on the other side of the garden fence.

But while Mary might have been safe from criticisms, she couldn't escape from curses. Grandma cursed if she jabbed herself with wire, or if she dropped the hammer, or if sweat dripped into her eye, or if a fly buzzed too close. And they weren't the tame, half-hearted swears that her dad sometimes used when he stubbed his toe.

They were terrible, dirty curses that managed to be both imaginative and to the point—and each time Mary felt her entire body tighten like a string on a violin, until she feared she'd snap if someone plucked her. She had never been around such coarse language in her entire life, and the ungodliness of it struck fear into her very soul.

At noon they went in for supper, and as Grandma predicted, Mary was hungry. Even with her spine held taut with offended anger, she was hungry. Beyond hungry even—ravenous.

They had ham sandwiches with great slices of lacy, delicate white cheese and a pile of spinach washed down with gulps of chilled apple cider. After, Grandma even produced some of her mother's iced sugar cookies—likely saved from that fateful day (though Mary noticed that there were no longer any white birds in the mix), and they dipped the fairies in milk for dessert.

Mary had never had such a delicious meal, despite it

being rougher, simpler fare than she was used to having at home.

Grandma Isabella, looking at her granddaughter over a second ham sandwich, thought she fancied a change in the girl already—a pinkness to her cheeks that was usually lacking. And without those hideous glasses obscuring them, her Ellmire eyes looked a very pretty shade of blue.

After supper, they sat by the wood stove and digested—Grandma Isabella believed firmly that digestion performed best in repose—and Mary tentatively asked if she might bring her quilt down and mend it.

Grandma nodded curtly and took up her own work. She was knitting a bright green blanket, the same color as moss when the sun shines through the canopy and lights it up. It was far too green and bright for Mary's tastes, but the pattern was pretty, and Grandma's fingers moved with a briskness that was to be admired.

They worked in comfortable silence, the only sound the snap and crackle of the newly chopped logs in the wood stove. When the sun began to set, they trooped out again into the chill air, this time to put the chickens away before nightfall and to give the cow her evening milking.

The cow was called Rosie. Her coat shined as bright as copper in the setting sun from the long brushings that Grandma gave her each evening, and she produced the frothiest, creamiest milk Mary had ever tasted—even though the Dennison's cow was reputed to have the best milk in town. Clearly, thought Mary, a proper comparison had never been done.

Rosie allowed Mary to milk her with patience in those liquid brown eyes, swinging her head back now and then to check on how things were proceeding. She was such a sweet, gentle creature that Mary delighted in settling her into her shed stall and tossing a leaf of the rich clover hay beneath her nose.

There was a cozy sense of all-tucked-in-ness in the shed, and Mary imagined that perhaps it was a similar feeling to tucking a child into bed. Not that she ever would have the opportunity, she reflected bitterly as she trooped back inside.

Any satisfaction with the day slipped away with that thought. Useful or not, she was still destinyless. Still doomed to life on the fringes of society, with an old infidel as her only companion.

The feeling worsened when Grandma cracked open a flagon of beer, which hissed and fizzed like a living creature. Mary could smell it from across the table—a stale, flat smell that made her think of alleyways and illicit meetings. It gave her a headache, and she had to turn her head to the side so that wafts of it didn't blow directly at her.

Mary hated to think what Pastor Primrose would say if he knew she was sitting with someone drinking a beer. And a woman at that! She shuddered.

"Grandma," she started tentatively, to take her mind off the smell of the beer, "I noticed a cheerful little cottage light out my window—I hadn't known you had a neighbor so far out here."

Grandma belched, and Mary caught a whiff of stale yeast. "That's my only real neighbor—Theodore Primrose," she said, and took another long draw of beer.

Mary's heart stuttered with fear. And to think she'd thought that little light cheerful! Now the glimmer of it would give her nightmares.

When at last Grandma finished the last swig of her foul beverage and went in to her room, Mary tiptoed upstairs to her bedroom. She peered out of her window, and the light gleamed back at her. It looked far too friendly to belong to Theodore Primrose. She felt almost sorry for it.

Nevertheless, she drew the moth-eaten curtains tight over the window, and shut her eyelids hard to block it out of her dreams.

HER TIME at Grandma's quickly fell into a rhythm—they started their day with a simple breakfast of porridge laced with dried berries, honey, and cream skimmed off the top of the pitcher, and then they did outdoor chores for the morning. By the fourth day of chopping, Mary's swollen palms had started to form calluses, and her cheeks had been chapped to a permanent pink from the wind.

The weather had begun to warm, and the first green weeds poked their heads above the soil, necessitating long hours spent on their knees, pulling them out by the roots and flinging them toward the woods.

Mary's most respectable grey dress grew dirty and frayed, and no amount of wringing would get the earth stains out of the skirt. But out here, Mary did not mind untidiness in her personal appearance quite so much—the only beings to observe it were Grandma, Rosie, and the chickens, and they didn't seem to mind as long as she did her work and brought regular lumps of sugar and scattered the seed in a timely manner.

She'd had to learn to adjust her tidiness in the house as well. When she first went to sweep the floor, reaching right into the corners and under all the furniture, Grandma stopped her up short.

"No, no!" She cried, watching all that gloriously magical

dust get deposited outside in the grass. "You must always leave at least a pinch of dust, so that when the sun shines in the windows, there's enough to dance in it."

Mary didn't sweep so thoroughly after that, and the next time the sun shone in the window, she was surprised to find that Grandma was right—the little bits of dust glowed in the sun, and reminded her of miniscule fairies, dancing on air. She thought that maybe after she returned home she wouldn't sweep in all of the corners of her bedroom quite so well.

But while in some ways Mary could adjust to this new style of living, in others she simply could not change. For one, Grandma bathed out in the stream behind the house, and sometimes would even walk up to the lake for a skinny dip of an evening. It wouldn't have been so bad if the lake were uninhabited, but Theodore Primrose's house was screened from her swimming spot by only a couple of willow trees.

"It does the body good to get a shock of cold every once in a while," Grandma told Mary one evening as she handed her clothes over so that they didn't get muddy on the bank. Mary stood very primly on solid ground, her eyes averted from Grandma Isabella's bony old body. Her own dress was buttoned all the way up to her throat.

"Come on in Mary, it'll do you good," she chided from the water.

Mary's spine stiffened at the mere suggestion that she toss her clothes off and gallivant naked outdoors. "It certainly will not," she said, jaw tight.

"Oh, get the broom handle out of your fanny and jump in!"

In her past life, just these words would have been enough to send Mary crying to her room. But now she had more shocking things to contend with. "I'll die before I swim naked!" Mary pronounced.

Finally, Grandma relented. "Wait until you keep yourself up at night with the smell," she grumbled. "Then you'll join me."

Mary only lifted her nose into the air. She didn't breathe freely again until Grandma had come out of the water and put her clothes back on. Imagine if Theodore Primrose had come out of his cabin and seen!

After that, she lugged a bucket of water up to her room and bathed shivering in the dark each night before bed, casting doleful looks at Grandma's door with every step of the sloshing bucket.

Normally she would have been horrified by this new spitefulness in herself, but she was tired and irritable, and it was much more difficult to control oneself when one had to deal with an equally irritable old woman.

Sleep hadn't come easily since that first, exhausted night in her new bed. She found the nighttime sounds in the country disconcerting. She imagined rats prowling in the shadows, waiting until she fell asleep before they rushed in to nibble on her flesh, and wild men gazing up through the darkness into her window.

On windy nights, Theodore Primrose's light would come alive, and cast long shadows on her walls. Some nights she'd wake gasping for air, sure that he was going to bang in the door at any moment and point that terrible gun of his at her.

Mary had never been one to imagine things like that before, and the change disconcerted her. It was much more convenient not to have an overactive imagination, especially when you lived out in the woods with only an old lady to protect your honor.

But for as close as Theodore Primrose lived, Mary still had yet to see any sign of him, save for the perpetual stream of smoke that issued from his chimney, and that staring yellow light.

On Thursday, four days into Mary's stay, Grandma sent her out to fetch some butter and cream. Mary stepped outside, and scanning the ground around the cabin, realized that she had never seen a cellar door.

"Grandma," she called, popping her head back inside. "Where do you keep the butter and cream?"

Her grandma clasped a hand to her forehead. "I plum forgot I hadn't shown you. This old thing is a sieve, you know." She commonly compared her brain to kitchen utensils. Some days it was a colander. Others, a leaky old pot. On good days, it was a sponge. "We'll have an expedition after breakfast and I'll show you the old spot."

They had a breakfast of overwintered apples sliced thin into wedges and walnuts, all drizzled with honey—which was delicious even without the cream and butter. Then Grandma Isabella pinned her royal purple walking cloak on, and Mary, following her lead, donned her own grey cloak. Paired together in the woods they appeared like walking shadows, melting from one patch of darkness to the next.

Grandma led her out beyond the garden and followed the brook to the west, away from the glimmering lake. The ground climbed steeply. Soon, great rugged boulders jutted up from the forest floor. Mary had no choice but to clamber over them.

The exercise brought an unfamiliar, but not unpleasant, warmth to her body. She loosened her hood so that it draped down around her shoulders, and her hair ripped free from its knot and the sunshine brought notes of auburn to it.

For the first time in her life, she felt beautiful. In the moment when she first noticed the loveliness of her body—of using her muscles for climbing and seeing and exploring—she found that she loved and was grateful for the strength in her limbs, for the sharpness of her eyes and the keenness of her senses.

Even the homeliest face is beautiful when it is lit up by self-respect.

It wasn't long before they heard a roar over the gentle babble of the stream. It reminded Mary of the grain mill, its giant gears grinding hard with the pull of the water, and when they broke through the trees, she was surprised to see not a mill, but a great spout of water that tumbled over a cliff and cascaded onto the rocks below. Brilliant rainbows formed in the droplets where it broke, shimmering and vanishing with the play of the water.

Grandma picked her way nimbly up the great boulders at the side of the waterfall, and Mary scrambled up behind her, grasping with both hands as she climbed, so as not to slip on the damp, mossy rocks.

Soon they reached the top, and without a word of instruction, Grandma disappeared behind a curtain of ivy. Mary was just small enough not to knock her head on the craggy ceiling as she stooped to follow.

A welcome draft of frigid air pressed against her neck. As Mary's eyes adjusted, she was able to make out the strange room.

Over the centuries the stream had carved a cave underneath the waterfall. And then the water had eroded the rocks below and it had moved on down the valley and left a dry, round cave, perfect for storing perishables.

Someone, perhaps even Grandma, had carved shelves into the rock. Mary saw jugs of milk and pots of cream and great rolls of cheese and butter. Large, round barrels of apples and potatoes and onions—half empty after the long winter—lined the opposite wall, and hunks of meat hung from the ceiling in tidy rows.

It was so wonderful that for a moment Mary forgot that she was destinyless and determined to mourn for the rest of her likely short life. "What a delightful spot," she exclaimed, picking up a molded butter pat in the shape of a rose. "All this is yours?"

Grandma was busy selecting a pot of cream and a wheel of butter. She tucked them up in the waxed linens she'd brought with her, like she was wrapping a present.

"I share it with Theo Primrose," Grandma said, in a tone that indicated it ought to be obvious. "He hunts for meat and I make the butter and cheese and milk—we have a good trade of it. He brought that rabbit the other week as a thanks for lending him my cookbook."

"Theodore Primrose?!" Mary repeated, astonished. She couldn't picture him doing anything as neighborly as borrowing a cookbook. "You mean the Theodore Primrose who shot his dog?"

Grandma's face grew sober. "The very same." She finished securing a second wheel of butter, and then led Mary out of the cave and back down the rocks.

They were silent as they walked through the woods, both caught up in their private thoughts.

"He really did shoot his dog?" Mary's mind was still on Theodore Primrose's wild, unaccountable ways. If anything, her fear of him had grown now that Grandma had affirmed the rumor.

"Yes, he did, in a moment of temper. He regrets it greatly now."

A temper. That was one of the worst attributes a person could have. At least it was in patient, quiet, Mary's book. Her pride still stung from her first day with Grandma, when she'd lost her temper and thrown her axe.

"It is not lady-like to lose your temper," she had used to

say primly when Delia was in a snit, which of course, only fanned the flames higher.

"I'll stay well away from that Theodore Primrose," she said to herself as she got ready for bed that night. It was the only sensible course to take.

Poor Mary couldn't know that Theodore Primrose had arrived home from a long hunting trip only the day before, and that her mettle on this matter would be tested the very next day.

Mary was out by the cowshed, brushing Rosie's coat to such a high gloss that she could nearly see her reflection in the coppery hairs, when the cow's ears twitched a hello.

She looked up to find Theodore himself, a book in his hands and a little red dog at his heels. He stood at the paddock gate, and Mary might've noticed his sheepish expression if his mouth hadn't been hidden in a great length of black winter beard.

Theodore Primrose had come for two reasons: to return the cookbook he'd borrowed from Grandma Isabella, and to satisfy his curiosity on the rumor that had been circulating for the past two weeks that Mary Ellmire's eyes had gone completely white.

This second point was immediately resolved: by the way she was glaring at him over the back of the cow, it was clear that they were functioning quite well. And not only were they functioning, but Mary had forgotten her glasses again, and the bright blue of her irises was rather prettier than Theo had ever noticed before.

"G'morning, Mary," he said comfortably. "Is Grandma Isabella about?"

Mary said something that wasn't audible above the burble of the stream.

"What was that? My hearing isn't the best—the curse of

growing up around guns, you know," he said it so good-naturedly, and his eyes were such a warm shade of chestnut brown, that Mary almost might have been in danger of losing her fear of him.

But then his dog shifted, and she noticed it was missing a hind leg, and that it hobbled as it walked, like a lame horse. It was one thing to shoot your dog, but another altogether to shoot its leg right off.

Mary felt such horror that she disappeared behind the cow, and after a moment Theodore shrugged and trooped off to the house to find Grandma Isabella on his own, thinking that while Mary Ellmire might not be blind, she was more than strange enough to make up for the disappointment.

Chapter Five

For two long weeks, Mary didn't hear a word from anyone in town. Her parents wanted to give her time to settle in, she supposed, but it stung that Delia hadn't come out to visit. So when the littlest Edelstein boy came trotting up with a rolled note in his hands, Mary clutched at it like a lifeline. She was so preoccupied with unrolling it that she didn't even notice the curious distance the boy gave her in handing it over, and the sidelong way he glanced into her face.

"Delia's sent for me to come to tea," she announced, in a positively gleeful tone—quite a contrast to her usually grim countenance—as she shooed the boy away with her answer.

Grandma looked up from her knitting. "It'll be good for you to get out of the house. Just mind you don't take anything those town turkeys say or do too much to heart."

But Mary didn't hear her. She was already buttoning the throat of her cloak.

It was odd to set out alone—even in full daylight the woods were shadowy and mysterious—but Mary didn't dare ask Grandma to walk her.

She wasn't sure that Grandma would take the hint and

leave them alone, and she was desperate to tell Delia every-thing, even if it wasn't proper to gossip. Even true ladies some-times need to share things with a friend, Mary reasoned as she walked, trying to assuage her guilt.

Soon she'd left the trees and hills behind and came onto the quaint cobblestone road that led into town. It wasn't until she reached the street and ran almost smack dab into Mrs. Hellman—one of the most esteemed church ladies, who gasped at the sight of Mary and then pasted on her best Church smile and hurried away—that Mary remembered she was a destinyless pariah.

The feeling of elation popped like a soap bubble. She drew her hood up firmly around her head and took a winding back alley the rest of the way to avoid any midday shoppers.

Clothes lines stretched across the street above her head, and a gang of children crouched on the ground around a toad that the eldest girl held proudly in her hands. As Mary passed, they all fell silent. She felt their gazes on her back all the way to the end of the alley.

Poor toad. Poor Mary.

Delia was already waiting for her inside the big glass window of the baker's shop. She'd ordered two mugs of choco-late. On a flower-patterned plate beside the mugs sat two fat jelly donuts dusted with a sprinkling of sugar.

"I took the liberty of ordering us refreshments," said Delia in her most sophisticated tone.

Mary pasted on a tremulous smile. It was so refreshing to have some refinement after a week with Grandma. Even pariahs deserved that, surely.

Delia looked especially sophisticated in her long blue dress with its puff sleeves. The dress was low enough that Mary could just see the golden cross her father had given her resting between her collarbones. She must be on to a new job —blacksmith Delia had never worn puff sleeves.

"Thank you," Mary said, and hesitated. Delia had chosen a table right in view of the street, and Mary already felt like a spectacle. But she was too polite to ask to move tables, and so she angled herself sideways so that her back faced the window. It was an uncomfortable position—her neck quickly became cramped—but at least she could remain blissfully ignorant of everyone who went by.

"Tell me all about it," said Delia as soon as they'd taken the first nibbles of their doughnuts. So Mary told her about everything from the skinny dipping to the wood chopping to the cursing.

Delia—not being half so proper as Mary—laughed as she listened to the tale. "I always knew Grandma Isabella was a mad woman," she said with satisfaction. She made a show of dabbing powdered sugar off of her lap, and then glanced slyly up at Mary again. "Speaking of mad people, have you seen that Theodore Primrose yet?"

"I—I haven't," said Mary after a guilty glance up at the counter—Theodore's second brother, Simon, had recently inherited the bakery. Besides, it seemed to her that her reputation had sunk enough just by being associated with Grandma. She didn't need Theodore Primrose wound up in it all as well.

"That's too bad. I've heard your grandmother is actually friends with him. Mark Dennison said he saw them puffing away on pipes together one evening when he was passing through to fish in the lake."

Mary blushed in embarrassment. "Well they haven't done such a thing while I have been there," she said quickly. "And hopefully it will stay that way."

"Hopefully," repeated Delia, though it came out sounding rather insincere.

"How has town been getting on without me?" Mary asked to change the subject.

Delia launched into the latest news—how her older sister, Cecilia was faring with her new baby (very poorly—she was always crying into supper when Delia went over), what the latest fashions were (pastel tones and quarter length sleeves), and who was soon to receive their destiny.

She'd started a new position at the green grocers', arranging displays of sweets and vegetables in the windows to lure shoppers inside.

Luckily for Mary, no one had had an eighteenth birthday since her own, and so she didn't have to hear any tales about luckier people than herself getting their little white birds.

However, Delia did relay that the whole of the town had been cast into uncertainty over the matter of her destiny not coming.

It seemed that many people felt that Mary's destinyless-ness signaled the end of destinies altogether. Delia's father was the leader of this faction. "They don't fit in the new world, with trains and plumbing and the mundane," he'd tell anyone who'd listen. "Mary was only the first to find out, poor soul."

But then, Mr. Trotter was also one of the people advocating for electricity, and everyone knew that that would never happen. Not in Tolling Bell.

Others thought that she'd just been unlucky, and that her bird had gotten lost or confused, or her parents had gotten her birthday wrong and the whole thing had been bungled from the beginning.

Mary wanted to believe this herself—that maybe it would still come yet. Some mornings the white flutter of wings bursting up through the canopy made her heart burst with such hope that it felt bruised when she realized they were only seagulls coming up from the roost.

Still a third group believed that Mary had done something wicked, and that was why her destiny hadn't come. That she was the subject of talk like this pierced her poor little soul so through with shame, she wished she could disappear on the spot. No wonder Mrs. Hellman had smiled so horrifically at her and run away.

She finished her donut and drained the last dregs of her tea quickly after Delia relayed this latest bit. She could feel the stares of everyone that passed by the window like flames on her back. Mary said goodbye to Delia and slunk out of the shop and back up the street like a dog that had been kicked.

Her mood was so dark when she arrived home that Grandma felt it darken the cottage as soon as she stepped through the door.

At this point tears had gathered in Mary's eyes like the first drops of rain in a thunderstorm, and she couldn't stop Grandma from seeing as they shook loose and ran down her cheeks.

"What ever is the matter?" Grandma's tone was perplexed. She'd only raised one child—Mary's father—and his tears had always come in great tantrums, complete with kicking and shouting and bellowing his pain out like a stuck pig. And despite all her years as headmistress of the school, the students had seldom come to her with their worries. Grandma Isabella was out of her depths when it came to silent tears. "Come here, child," she said at last, and extended her arms.

Mary obeyed, and half sank onto her lap on the rocking chair. "I'm sorry," she said with a sniffle, and tried to wipe the tears away. That only seemed to bring them on more.

"Maybe you should just let them come," said Grandma after a moment. "It's like trying to stop a rainstorm."

So Mary let the tears come, and told her in snotty gasps all that Delia had told her about what the town people thought of her.

Grandma's fists clenched as she listened. "I'd like to skewer them all through with a pitchfork," she said when Mary finished talking. "But as that would only embarrass you more, I won't."

She leaned back and looked her granddaughter in the face. "There may not be much you can learn from me, Mary. I am old and coarse and far less patient than I ought to be. But if I have anything worth emulating, it is not caring a wink about what other people think about me."

"I do care, though," Mary wailed piteously.

"Why?" roared Grandma back at her. "Would you rather be someone wicked who everyone thinks is good, or someone good who everyone thinks is wicked? People are often wrong, and you can't control what they think of you. So instead of worrying about whether they think you are good or bad, focus instead on trying to be who you want to be."

That stopped Mary up short. It was a good point for someone like Mary Ellmire, who valued morality and self-improvement as much as propriety. She sniffled as she considered.

"I suppose you are right," she began haltingly.

"I'm damn right!" declared Grandma. She patted Mary on the shoulder. "Now go up and sleep away your weepies. You'll feel better for it."

Mary took her advice and retreated up to her bedroom to ponder the matter.

This bit of wisdom cast a new light on Grandma's actions, and made guilt bubble in her gut for all of the unkind things she'd said to Delia that morning. As she sat on her bed in the dark, more and more kindnesses occurred to her—good things that Grandma did along with the improper ones. Sure, she may drink beer and never attend church and swim naked at dusk, but she grew vegetables and knit blankets for the poor and watched children for townspeople who needed to go out of town for the day.

The next morning, as Grandma milked Rosie, Mary watched out of the corner of her eye—noting the way she spoke to the cow in low soothing tones, and stroked one of her long, velveteen ears goodbye as thanks for the milk as she left. The cow nodded her head peaceably and set into the fresh leaf of hay that had been fluffed in front of her nose.

It was quite a contrast to how the Dennison's treated their cow—tersely, with sharp yanks on the lead and jabs from their pointy elbows. Mary decided that if she should ever have her own cow, she would take a leaf out of Grandma's book.

When they set to weeding, Mary watched as Grandma got down on her hands and knees—carefully plucking out the seedling imposters and stroking the garden plants with gentle fingers.

Mary's back always ached after only an hour of weeding. She had never thought how tired Grandma's must get—but she never said a word of it hurting, and only cursed at the occasional mosquito.

Just before noon, Mr. Wistman appeared at the garden gate—his family was one of the poorest in town. They lived over the railroad tracks, in the cluster of wind-battered, grey houses where the poor folks carved out their rough existence. A little boy clutched at his hand, his eyes wide as he watched Mary and Grandma.

Grandma stood at once and brushed off her hands. "Apologies for the dirt," she said, and hurried out of the gate.

Mr. Wistman started to speak—after a quick, embarrassed glance at Mary—but Grandma cut him off. "Come in for a cuppa. Can't have a proper conversation without refreshments, can we?"

As they walked away, Mary heard her say to the little boy, "Perhaps you can taste-test Rosie's latest batch of milk for me. I'm sure I can rustle up some cookies for you to dip in it."

It wasn't long before Mr. Wistman and the little boy reappeared. The boy had let go of his father's hand and skipped ahead on the path—squatting to investigate a grasshopper before leaping away again in a near imitation of it.

Mr. Wistman carried a loaf of bread under one arm— the one that Grandma had put in the oven only that morning for their dinner—a wheel of cheese, and a second jug of milk. When Mary went inside, she found a knit hat on the table, its undyed yarn blending with the silvery wood.

"I thought you might keep that hat for winter," Grandma said without looking up. "Mr. Wistman's wife knitted it."

Mary picked it up thoughtfully, feeling the soft wool under her fingers. "Did he give it in exchange for the food?"

"Yep." Grandma had her back to her, her hands busy as she briskly washed a bowl.

"Why did you accept it?" Mary asked, surprised.

Grandma looked up sharply at that. "You'll see when you come around on vegetable deliveries with me this summer. People don't want charity. They want neighbors. If I hadn't let Mr. Wistman leave me this hat, he would've left shamed. And then next time his family was hungry, he wouldn't have come. It's best to leave people their dignity."

She gazed hard at Mary, to make sure the lesson had sunk in. In reply, Mary slid the hat over her ears. "Well, how does it look?"

Grandma's face softened with a smile. "It looks marvelous."

When they went back outside that afternoon, Mary found herself chatting away to Grandma—asking about the birds that visited the feeder while they were gardening, or how to tell the difference between the earliest shoots and weeds.

Grandma just smiled into the ground as she worked, and pointed out the tiny differences in the plants. And when a new bird fluttered to the feeder, she made sure to stop and tell Mary all about it—whether it was a regular or a visitor, where it might nest, and what sorts of seeds it preferred.

She'd never found another person so easy to talk to—Delia always had so much to say that Mary usually just listened. And her mother was too curious, too desperate to know her every thought. It made her quiet, afraid that she might somehow disappoint.

But there was something about Grandma's gruff silences—silences that made Mary feel as though she wouldn't have given a hoot if Mary announced she wanted to go to the moon—that invited confidence. And her insights into what Mary had to say were always so funny and unexpected—full of wisdom and spice and humor.

Mary still blushed when Grandma kicked her legs up after dinner so that her petticoats fell back to reveal skinny white legs. But she no longer felt like she might melt right into the ground with embarrassment. And she found Grandma's swearing much more bearable when paired with all the nice things she'd said throughout the day.

By Mary's third week at Grandma's house, she had mended the pile of quilts on her bed, and sewn in patches of flannel and denim where the holes were too large to sew back together. Now the quilts no longer looked like childhood relics that had been loved and forgotten, but had an air of being cared for still. It lent a very warm feeling to the loft, and along with the wreath and a vase of purple crocus that had bloomed outside the cottage, it was beginning to feel very much like home.

THAT SUNDAY, Mary decided that she would brave the stares of Tolling Bell to attend church. She'd missed three whole Sunday services—the longest period she'd gone in her entire life without attending one, and the ease with which she'd missed it worried her. It seemed to Mary that she ought to need God more than ever now that she was destinyless.

Grandma attended in solidarity with her, though she wasn't pleased about breaking her churchless streak of some dozen years. She grumbled the whole way there—her hip was hurting and it was a bit of a walk (though downhill), and besides, the garden was beginning to flourish and needed long hours of tending to grow to its best.

"Grandma," began Mary tentatively, when the complaints of the long walk reached a pitch she worried might carry up to the church itself (the squadron of church ladies were known for having particularly sharp ears). "Why did you move so far outside of town, if you hate the long walk into it?"

Grandma Isabella cast her a sharp look. "I taught school for fifty years, and was married to your grandfather for forty-nine. When I finally had a chance to escape from all that destiny, I thought I'd better escape it as well as I could."

Mary frowned. Grandma almost made it sound like having a destiny was a bad thing. But how could it be, when it provided a loving husband and son and a fulfilling career, and everything that she so yearned for out of life?

As they entered the church, dozens of eyes lifted to her face, and then flitted automatically away—like shooed flies. Mary lifted her chin, and thought about what Grandma had said about true goodness. The words were like armor over her tender heart—though a blush still did rise to her cheeks when one of the little Hellmans pointed at her.

It helped to have a whole new question to ponder. Escape. You escaped from bandits and spooks. Not from your destiny. It was quite a mystery to Mary why anyone would ever want to escape their destiny.

She sat down in the usual pew, with her parents on one side and Delia and her family on the other. With Grandma there it was more crowded than usual, but Mary hardly noticed. She was so busy puzzling over what Grandma had said that she soon forgot the eyes upon her back, and Pastor Primrose's stern admonishment during his sermon to 'Think hard upon your sins and repent, or fair fortune shall not find you' passed right over her head.

It was good she didn't hear it, because that sort of criticism from such an esteemed community member would have quenched any of the thirst for life that she had begun to build up over the last few weeks.

Afterwards they had a picnic in the apple orchard beside the church, and her parents and Delia joined them for a repast of goat cheese and thick, nutty bread slathered with honey. Delia had brought roasted nuts from their walnut tree the year prior, and her mother supplied sugar cookies, decorated as blooming flowers in pastel shades of pink and orange, with a large pitcher of foamy milk.

Mary's parents were amazed to watch as their daughter consumed slice after slice of bread, each smothered with cheese and dripping with honey, and then rounded the whole meal off by saturating her share of cookies with milk and eating those too. Not only that, but she'd stopped wearing those infernal glasses, and her cheeks had a flush to them.

This alone was enough to convince them that they'd made the right decision sending her to Grandma's, even if Aunt Moore had been very critical, and if Pastor Primrose had declared that Mary would undoubtedly become that most terrible of things: an infidel.

Townsfolk on their way home from the service stopped in to say hello and wish Mary well—though Tommy Edelstein really just wanted to get a better glimpse of Mary's eyes, and to be honest, so did the farmer, Mr. Thomas. Her father's glower told each person they'd better not say anything about destinies or lack thereof.

Augustus Primrose even paused as he walked past. He nodded at Mary's parents and cast a tight wave toward Delia before walking stiffly back up to the church.

That was a blow to poor Mary, who had been as unacknowledged as the apple trees. Grandma Isabella had also been ignored, but if anything it seemed to amuse her.

"Primpy little shrimp, isn't he?" she said gleefully as she bobbed a pink sugar cookie in milk.

Mary smiled—she couldn't help it. And she was so busy smiling that she missed the worried glance that her parents passed between themselves. But they held their tongues—it was the first time they'd seen Mary's lips so much as twitch since her birthday. And she did look very healthy—was it really so bad for a little bit of Grandma to rub off on her?

So Mary remained oblivious to their fears, and her good mood held. She even went as far as to link an arm with Grandma Isabella as they walked back to the cottage, so as to ease the strain on her hip.

Chapter Six

THEY ARRIVED home to a note tacked on the door. The handwriting was spiky and small, as though the writer had only had an inch of room, rather than an entire sheet.

Deer down. Steak for dinner? Mushrooms would suit nicely.

-TVP

Grandma plucked it off the door. The fatigue of the morning seemed to wash off of her as she read it. "Steak! Mushrooms certainly would suit," she said to herself. "And perhaps some wine. Come along then Mary, we've got mushrooms to collect! We'll leave him an answer on our way."

And off they trotted, Mary wondering what in the world it all meant. A feeling of dread had settled low in her stomach. She surmised that TVP must be Theodore Primrose, though she wasn't certain of the middle initial. How could she stand to sit through an entire dinner with such an infernal person?

Grandma strode so quickly through the woods—her aching hip forgotten—that Mary had to jog to catch up.

It wasn't long before the lake broke through the trees. The sunlight bouncing off of its surface was so brilliant that Mary blinked several times before she could make out the cabin perched on its shore. Towering pine trees wrapped it in a pine-needled hug, and the front porch nearly hung over the water.

The entire scene spoke of long, slow days spent with toes dangling in the lake. A "roo roo" of a bark alerted them to the red dog's presence. It was curled up in a patch of sun on the porch, its fluffy ears at alert.

"Hello, Sparrow old girl," said Grandma as she stomped up the stairs. The dog wagged her tail furiously, and Grandma patted her head with an age-spotted hand.

Despite herself, Mary reached down to stroke an ear. It was ridiculously silky against the newfound calluses on her fingers.

On closer inspection, Sparrow was a beautiful dog, with rich red fur coating her body in a series of gentle waves, and snowy legs (excepting, of course, the right hind, which was missing).

Her tail was perhaps prettiest of all, thick and luscious, with a white tip at the end as if it had been dipped in paint.

"Theodore!" Grandma shouted through the open door. Inside, Mary could just make out a miniature stone fireplace, with a great lumpy green couch in front of it. A black cat laid on the back of the sofa, its tail twitching as it eyed them through wicked gold eyes. On the back wall, dozens of books lined an unvarnished shelf.

Mary was so busy trying to get a peek inside that she didn't notice when the answering "halloa!" came from around the side of the cottage, and Theodore Primrose appeared suddenly at the rail. She jumped.

He tipped his straw sunhat to Mary, and then fixed his steady gaze on Grandma Isabella. "Steak for dinner, then?"

"We're on our way to rustle up some mushrooms now," Grandma said. "Should be back before too long, it's the right time for mushrooms."

"Certainly is," Theodore agreed. "We'll trot along shortly then."

Mary wondered who we was, until she noticed the dog sitting up and licking her chops as she looked between Grandma and Theodore—like she had been a participating member in the conversation.

Theodore waved at Mary as she followed Grandma down the porch steps and into the woods again, and Mary—having trained herself to be the picture of politeness—waved automatically back.

His answering grin sent a jolt of fear through her spine. How, oh how, was she to survive in the same room as him?

The dread of dinner weighed on her as they collected mushrooms, though Mary couldn't help enjoying the task itself. It reminded her of her childhood, when they'd had egg hunts through the apple orchard every Easter. She'd always been good at spying hidden eggs with her sharp eyes, and back when she'd allowed herself to do such things, had been particularly adept at shimmying to the highest branches to fetch the hard ones.

Now she proved equally skilled at spying out the brown, wrinkle-topped mushrooms they were collecting. Grandma had stopped her in the beginning, when she'd gone to pick a shiny red-capped one that looked like a toadstool a fairy might sleep under.

"Never pick an unfamiliar mushroom!" Grandma

scolded, so ferociously that tears sprang to Mary's eyes. "You'll be dead faster than that—" and with a snap of her fingers and a stomp of her booted foot, she showed Mary exactly how quickly she'd be dead.

But then she softened and smiled a bit, and showed her what to look for in the proper sort of mushroom—the brown color, bumpy shape, and hollow interior. Soon Mary was spotting clusters of them all through the forest, especially below the ridge-leaved elm trees that Grandma said fostered mushrooms with the decay in their roots.

When they had enough, Grandma brought her to a clearing and showed her how to pick the newly sprouted dandelion greens. "They're tenderest early in the season, but with a good long boil and some salt and butter, they make mighty fine forage through the summer."

Before long Grandma's satchel was full. Mary hoisted it on her own back as they walked homeward. She was rather excited about eating the mushrooms and greens—never before had she harvested her food from the wild. There was something lovely in the idea that this bounty existed right outside their door, ready to nourish without asking anything in return. It lent her a hunger quite apart from her own.

Theodore was already waiting when they came back through the paddock gate. He leaned against the tall oak tree outside Mary's bedroom window, his long legs stretched out in the grass. Sparrow's head rested on his foot, though she raised it to greet them with her little "roo roo!"

At that he opened his eyes and sprang to his feet, his height growing suddenly from the ground as he straightened. He carried a thick package of waxy white paper in one hand, and a dusty bottle in the other. As his eyes met Mary's, she felt her cheeks flush a vicious red.

"Simon sent along some of his best plum wine from the

bakery," he said, holding the bottle out to Grandma. "Said it was a shame to have venison without a good wine." Simon was the second eldest Primrose—he'd turned eighteen only a few months before Mary. She'd grown up going to school with him, though he was quieter than a fawn in a thicket.

According to town talk, he'd gotten his destiny to take over the bakery from old Mr. Mellwood only two weeks before the old man had passed away, leaving Simon in a lurch as he tried to learn the trade.

"He's certainly right." Grandma led them inside and popped the cork of the bottle unceremoniously while Theodore unwrapped the white package. Inside lay a small log of meat, with butcher's twine holding it artistically together. It was a luscious, velvety red—far redder and richer than the pale steaks her father sometimes brought home from the butcher. Sparrow danced at his feet with joy at the sight of it, her dark eyes sparkling.

Theodore cracked pepper on it and rubbed small blue berries into the flesh that smelt of pine and citrus, and then they stoked the stove until the skillet sizzled with heat. The meat crackled and spat as he laid it down, and before long it had filled the entire house with a smell so wonderful that a string of drool fell from Sparrow's mouth.

At first Mary hid behind the stove, pretending to fiddle with one thing and then another. But then Grandma called her over to where she was rinsing and chopping the mushrooms and greens. She set Mary to peeling gigantic cloves of garlic and slicing them so fine that they shone translucent in the afternoon sun streaming in through the kitchen window.

Mary obeyed, but she kept her eyes firmly on the cutting board, her every nerve aware of where Theodore stood in the kitchen in relation to her.

When the steaks were ready to come out, Grandma tossed

the vegetables in the rich juice they had left behind, and cut thick hunks of butter to melt in the pan. Soon the mushrooms were a deep brown and the greens glistened.

Theodore meted it all out onto four rough earthenware plates, and Grandma poured out three mugs of plum wine, and then they carried the bounty out to the oak tree and ate Sunday dinner in the long grass.

Sparrow waited politely until the others cut into their steaks before she wolfed her own down in three big bites, and then she nibbled the greens and mushrooms a bit more daintily. Mary had never tasted anything so delicious. It was so good that she momentarily forgot her fear of Theodore—the steak was so tender that she barely needed her knife to cut it into strips. The flavor was smoky and woodsy and piney.

It tasted like a creature that had lived a happy life beneath the trees growing sweet and plump on acorns, instead of in a slaughterhouse. And while she hadn't meant to drink more than a sip of the wine, it was so deep and fruity that before she knew it, she'd drained her glass.

Grandma and Theodore kept up an easy chatter, discussing the weather and the growing conditions, and when Grandma's tomatoes might begin to put out fruit. And then Theodore entertained them with stories about Simon's foibles in trying to fix up the old cabin on the lake he'd inherited from old Mr. Mellwood, and how he constantly misplaced hammers and put doors on backwards and forgot to close windows, so that families of raccoons took up residence in the outhouse and under the porch.

He was an artist with spun sugar, Theodore told them, his mouth twisting with affection for his subject, "And as scattered as a squirrel in spring."

Mary was entertained despite herself—Theodore was a funny, good-hearted narrator, and it was hard not to root for witless Simon in his mission to fix up the old house on the lake. However, she kept to her resolution not to speak with him and avoided his eye whenever he directed a particularly funny part of a story toward her.

After dinner, Mary washed while Grandma dried and Theodore put away. Sparrow stayed out from underfoot by curling up in Grandma's favorite chair and taking a nap. Mary was scandalized to see how well Theodore knew his way around Grandma's kitchen—his hands automatically placed the mugs in their proper homes, and he knew just how to stack the plates so that they all fit.

Then Theodore and Sparrow went away, and it was just Grandma and Mary again. The house felt quiet and empty without them. Mary thought about striking up a conversation with Grandma just to fill the silence. But all she could think about was Theodore—why he lived so far out in the woods, how he had come to be so strange, and why he had shot that sweet little dog of his—and her nerve failed her.

Instead, she went upstairs to bed. She wasn't tired yet, even though her body was full and sluggish from the delicious meal.

MARY SOON LEARNED that Sunday dinners with Theodore Primrose were a regular ritual in Grandma's house. They didn't always have venison steak—most days Theodore wasn't lucky enough to get a deer. But they always had something scrumptious—a kidney pie with great heaps of mashed potatoes, or a hearty salad of dandelion greens and grilled fish. Afterwards he entertained them with tales of life's going ons.

Her fear of him began to fade slightly—she no longer

woke in the middle of the night gasping and drenched in sweat, terrified that he was at the front door with a gun. It was hard to be afraid of someone who chattered so amiably about things like wildflowers and bird song. Plus, fearful imaginings tend to thrive best in the dark, and their Sunday dinners were always so full of light and good food.

Still though, she kept quietly to herself when he came about, and did her best to avoid his gaze. Somehow she couldn't bring herself to treat him normally—it felt like a betrayal to all that she had been for her entire life just to have dinner with him. And besides, there was the matter of his temper to keep a spark of fear alive in her heart.

Theodore began to split in her mind: there was the terrible Theodore Primrose who had shot Sparrow. And then there was Theo, their neighbor, who told jolly stories and was a wonderful cook, and who seemed to be Grandma's one true friend in the world.

Sometimes, on her long walks to church on Sunday mornings, she tried to imagine why he had shot Sparrow. But her imagination couldn't dredge up any reason why he'd have wanted to shoot the sweet little dog—no reason seemed to justify the act. And as she got to know Sparrow better, and to love her soft ears and big, dark eyes, and the way she'd rest her chin on your knee to beg for attention, the crime only grew more heinous.

There was much to ponder in her new life—Theodore, and church, and Grandma's feelings about her own destiny.

Mary had always thought that Grandma had had a wonderful destiny—her own esteemed grandfather to marry, with his wondrous mustache, and a respectable job as headmistress of the school. It was one of the most respectable careers in town, and many boys and girls dreamed of having it one day.

But Grandma seemed happy now. Certainly much happier than when Mary had been a child, and she had scolded for things like climbing trees and forgetting to use her inside voice. The old Grandma most certainly wouldn't have cared for dust in her motes of sunshine, or had Sunday dinners with someone as wild as Theodore Primrose. Perhaps when you had lived out your destiny, you were free to do what you wanted. And now Grandma was doing what she wanted.

Still, Grandma had been lucky to have a destiny at all, even if it wasn't exactly what she would've wanted. Mary felt that she would give almost anything for her own destiny—she'd even have happily lived in a musty old cabin out in the woods with the town reprobate, if only a white bird had told her it was the right thing to do.

Chapter Seven

WHILE GRANDMA HAD BEEN willing to accompany Mary to church that first time, she'd declared that one visit with God in twelve years was more than enough when Mary had asked the next week.

At first Mary had been nervous to walk alone. She jumped at every small sound, and constantly scanned the underbrush to make sure no monsters lurked there. Having time alone to imagine things like monsters was a new experience for Mary. She'd always been accompanied by her parents before coming to grandma's house.

But after those first few, nervous walks, she got used to walking alone. She came to find that there was something thrilling about strolling through the woods with her picnic basket—which contained lunch for herself and Delia.

Alone, she could imagine herself as Red Riding Hood from the fairy tale, cleverly evading the wolf. Or Gretel searching for dropped crumbs.

She could even imagine that she had a destiny—a grand one—and would save the town from poachers and marry the most handsome man in the village, who had mysteriously changed from being mustached and slim shouldered to having broad shoulders and very warm brown eyes.

She'd never had much of an imagination before this, but it seemed as though sunshine and solitary walks were the fuel her mind had been waiting for, and now it had blossomed at last.

With her newfound imagination came newfound freedom. She started taking long evening walks through the woods, losing herself to the thickets of wildflowers, and finding that the glowing, fluffy grass heads in fields were as magical as eddies of dust in sunshine, if not more so.

Some days she'd find her way back to her parents' house— for though she was beginning to enjoy her new life (as much as a destinyless person can enjoy anything), she missed them dearly. They'd welcome her in for a cup of tea and a bite of supper, and the three of them would have a nice little evening together.

On her first visit back, Mary had been very nervous to see the place of her acute misery. But the house was just as it had been before her eighteenth birthday—familiar and tidy and comfortable. Only the empty plaque waiting for her scroll had disappeared.

In ways, its disappearance made Mary even sadder than if it had stayed there, empty. That wooden plaque had waited for her fortune since she was born, and now it had disappeared as though she had never been supposed to receive a destiny at all.

But she'd put on a cheerful face and forced herself to clean her plate of shepherd's pie— even if her stomach had shrunk so much that she could hardly fit anything in it.

For their part, her parents had been very relieved when she turned up. It's a daunting thing to turn your child loose in the world for the very first time. Each of them had held a small slice of fear in their hearts that she'd take wing and never come back. But come back she did, and she was still their beloved Mary—even if she did laugh a little bit more loudly and if her skirts were a touch more frayed.

It was a relief for Mary to return to the cottage after her visits into town. Out there, her thoughts had room to bloom and grow, tucked safely away from the opinions of the towns-folk. After she got back, she'd always linger outside to stroke Rosie and greedily inhale the sweet, nighttime air.

As the summer wore on, thickets of raspberries and blue-berries bloomed in the woods out back, and the garden began to produce gorgeous red tomatoes and vines of thick green zucchini with hairs that glistened with dew each morning. Mary especially loved the look of the lacy shoots of kale and chard, which waved like cheerful banners from the ground.

She spent much of her days weeding and harvesting. Dirt was a permanent fixture under her fingernails, and her lips were often stained pink by the large volume of raspberries she consumed right off the vine. The fresh fruits and vegetables turned their meals into riotous delights of color and flavor.

One Sunday, as she went to don her primmest, non-stained dress for Church she noticed that it had become snug in the arms, and tight in the chest and hips. She'd put a padding of muscle and fat over her bones from all the hard work and good food.

Mary was, despite herself, delighted. She'd always wished that she was fat—someone had once told her that babies cried less when they had fat mothers, because they could better nestle in for a snuggle. And Mary desperately wanted to be a mother. It was ironic indeed that she'd finally become fat when it seemed least likely she'd ever become a mother.

The next day Grandma, noticing that Mary was beginning to fill out her clothes, took her into town to buy materials for new dresses.

"It's summer!" Grandma Isabella exclaimed as Mary fingered linen the color of tree bark.

"It's unnatural to wear colors so somber in summer. You'll look like you're in mourning. How about some rose? They'll be blooming soon. And this raspberry is simply lovely—it calls to mind the ripest fruits on the bush."

The only color Mary completely refused was an ochre that grandma pronounced the "Prettiest shade of yellow she'd ever seen."

"I'll look like an egg yolk," Mary grumbled, and after that Grandma didn't press the matter.

Mr. Bright, the shopkeeper, had watched in astonishment as the old lady talked dowdy, destinyless Mary Ellmire into his most fashionable colors.

At the checkout he asked, "Are you quite sure?"

Grandma pinioned him with her most eagle-eyed glare and paid for the lot in fat gold coins that she'd produced from some mysterious place out by the well.

So Mary walked away with the softest green linen, yard after yard of rosy pink cotton, and a sheer raspberry fabric that would make an enchanting formal dress—if only Grandma Isabella could convince her to make it up the way she had in mind. She had talked Grandma into getting one plain material—linen in a deep charcoal grey—which would hide stains well and be light enough for working in the garden.

As they walked back up to the cottage, they ran into Theodore on the path into town, his meat cart rattling behind him.

"On the way to the butcher?" Grandma inquired as they passed.

"Time to refill the coffers," Theodore said, eyes crinkling. He eyed the bundles of fabric overflowing from Mary's arms. "And it looks like you've got the makings for some new dresses —lovely choice of colors. Brings to mind spring in the garden."

"Don't bring it up," said Grandma rather shortly. "It took the whole of the morning to talk her into anything other than grey and brown."

Mary frowned severely at Grandma, who gazed unrepentantly back.

Theo grinned at Mary. "Well, I'm sure you'd look dashing in anything. Yellow's my personal favorite, though I'm never brave enough to wear it. Perhaps I should."

Mary smiled, and in a sudden surge of bravery, found herself saying, "Mr. Bright has an ochre that Grandma was quite sure I simply *needed*. Perhaps you should buy it yourself and make a shirt."

Theodore and Grandma met eyes briefly—was it Mary's imagination, or did Grandma look slightly guilty? "Well, we'd better keep moving," said Grandma after a moment. "We've got a lot of work ahead of us."

Theo's mouth quirked in a lopsided smile, and he caught Mary's gaze accidentally before trundling off into the woods with his cart.

The sewing of the dresses turned out to be another boon in Grandma's mission of un-reforming poor Mary, because she'd stumbled on one of the only points that could rise Mary to argue with her.

"You can't do tight sleeves. It isn't the fashion, and besides you need to be able to move your arms when we're working in the garden," Grandma would say, a glimmer of mischief in her eye.

And Mary's lips would disappear all together and she'd say nothing for long moments, until finally she'd burst out—"I shan't wear a sleeveless dress! It isn't decent and I shan't do it!"

They'd go back and forth like that until finally Grandma slyly suggested they compromise by making the rose cotton into a short-sleeved gown with white lace peeking out over the elbows, and Mary couldn't argue with that, because her mother insisted that the ability to compromise was the marker of a true lady.

If she couldn't have a destiny, at the very least she could still be a lady—even if it did mean wearing more modern dresses. And besides, the way Grandma described her vision of gowns that had the sweep of wild autumn leaves caught in a gale, and flowers just burst forth from the branch *did* sound lovely.

One sunny afternoon, Mary was picking raspberries in the woods—wearing her new rose colored dress—and Grandma and Theodore were sitting on rockers they'd dragged out into the sunshine, when Sparrow gave her familiar "roo roo!" from her patch in the sunshine.

Before long, Delia came up the path with a loaf of fresh bread in the nook of her arm. She'd grown curious hearing her friend's tales of life in the cottage, and had come to see for herself if Rosie's coat really glowed like burnished copper, and if the brook really was the sweetest water in all of Tolling Bell.

The one thing Mary still hadn't told her about, however, was of their association with Theodore Primrose. His wildness still embarrassed her, and she didn't need his own bad reputation darkening what remained of her own.

Delia stopped short on the path when she saw him, rocking merrily away with Grandma, his flannel shirt open at the collar and a pipe between his lips. He gave her a friendly wave as she passed, and Mary even caught him glance after her admiringly.

Delia did cut quite a figure in her sleeveless sapphire dress, which echoed the color of the lake's sparkle through the trees and the cloudless sky above. For an instant Mary felt hurt. But why? Mary didn't care a hoot who Theodore looked at, and she certainly wouldn't want him to look at her that way.

Would she?

The question troubled her as she and Delia exchanged kisses. Her friend followed her eagerly into the cottage as Mary went to fetch some sliced venison and horseradish left over from the evening before to eat the bread with, and a quilt from her room to sit upon.

The cabin was as Mary had described it, only cozier, and with a timeless charm that Delia had trouble believing the old reprobate had it in her to cultivate.

As they passed Grandma and Theodore, Grandma shouted, "Good to see you, Delia! I've been wondering when you'd visit Mary."

Delia smiled her most dignified smile, and nodded her most dignified nod, but didn't say anything more. When they'd spread their blanket out in the field, she cast a haughty glance back at the pair of them. "It is good you keep your distance from that man," she said. "Grandma Isabella is wild enough, but that Theodore Primrose is simply vicious."

Mary felt suddenly very hot in her charcoal work dress. She'd thought Grandma crazy often enough before she'd come to live in the cottage, but it was somehow different for Mary to think it than for Delia to say it.

"Grandma isn't exactly wild—" she ventured.

Delia laughed. "She's the wildest grandma I've ever met, tramping through the woods and boiling up concoctions."

Mary could feel heat creeping up into her cheeks. Those

things might seem wild, but she now knew that it took quite a lot of sense and propriety to get anything edible from nature.

After all, you couldn't know which mushrooms were poisonous and which were not if you lacked good sense. She told Delia as much, and Delia snorted derisively.

That snort was the last straw.

"Why, you don't know anything about Grandma, to be calling her wild!" flared Mary. "She might do things her own way, but it is always with good sense. And Theodore might have a temper, but—" she faltered. She really couldn't excuse his temper.

Delia's dark eyes flashed, and she seized on Mary's hesitation. "Any man who goes trooping about the woods, shooting poor animals and skinning them must be vicious! And that isn't even to mention the fact that he shot his own dog." She had a slice of bread layered with venison halfway to her mouth.

"And here you are, eating one of those poor animals without a second thought for the life behind it," Mary said, searing heat in her tone—though of course Delia was *right*. How could Theodore have shot that poor, sweet little dog? It seemed so contrary to the man she was slowly coming to know. But her anger was at a full boil now, and there was no stopping it. "And I've seen you eating steaks and roast chicken and pork, and all of those animals were raised up only to be slaughtered in stalls and barnyards, while Theodore's animals live lovely lives in the forest up until their deaths. I ought to call you vicious!"

Delia put down her bread abruptly. She and Mary had never quarreled so, because Mary had always been unwilling to lose her temper. "The way you carry on, I'd think you actually liked him!" She said, changing her attack.

It worked. "I don't like him!" Mary said, and lost it all

together. She gave Delia one furious, teary-eyed glare before stalking away to the barnyard, where she cried long, deep sobs into Rosie's silky red neck until Delia went away.

Then she slunk back to the field, only to find the quilt and food and dishes had disappeared. Grandma had disappeared as well—likely to the garden to check some matter or the other, and Theodore was inside, washing up the plates that Mary and Delia had used. He had shaken the quilt free of grass, and it was now folded neatly on one of the rockers. Sparrow was finishing the rest of Delia's sandwich.

"Thank you," said Mary, shyly.

"You're welcome," Theodore said, his brown eyes dark and very kindly in the shadowy cabin. "I hope all is okay between you and your friend."

Mary sighed. "I expect it will be, once I apologize to her tomorrow. I shouldn't have lost my temper."

Theo's mouth quirked up, as though the idea of Mary losing her temper was rather appealing. He wanted to ask what they had argued about—the whole scene had been visible from the rockers—but held his tongue.

Presently, Mary ventured, "You don't think Grandma is wild, do you?" She wasn't sure why she cared for his opinion at all—being a wild man himself, his thoughts on the matter couldn't really count, but she needed validation from someone.

"Not at all! Your grandma simply goes her own way. It's refreshing, after all of the bother that the people in town get up to. Grandma Isabella doesn't care what's proper. She only cares what's right. It's why she does things like bring vegetables to the poor on Sundays, and hand out blankets in wintertime."

Mary nodded solemnly. What he said rang true with all that she'd come to know in the last weeks. Her grandmother was overflowing in true goodness, and she herself had had it wrong for a very long time.

She smiled at him, this time with real warmth and only a little politeness. "Thank you, Theo."

Theodore was taken aback by how pretty she was when she smiled—her teeth were just crooked enough to be charming.

At that moment, Grandma Isabella herself came in with an armload of radishes that needed to be rinsed. That put an end to the conversation, and before long Theo went away into the shadowy woods with Sparrow loping at his heels.

Chapter Eight

THE NEXT DAY, Mary packed a basket full of sugar cookies that she'd baked herself—these ones white hearts with ripe raspberries pressed into the frosting—and a jug of Rosie's freshest, sweetest milk, and walked into town to apologize to Delia.

She knocked on the bright blue door of the sprawling house Delia and her parents lived in, and Delia's mother took one glance out and said she'd get her daughter. Delia's mother and father were very good sort of people—both by town standards and Grandma standards—they went to church every Sunday, and whenever anyone was ill they would bring a vat of their famous chicken soup.

Presently, Delia came out of the front door. Mary sat down upon their porch swing, her booted toes sweeping the floor with each swing, and gestured for Delia to sit beside her. "I'm sorry I lost my temper yesterday," Mary said. "Grandma has been so good to me—and Theodore hasn't said an unkind word—so your words stung and I felt defensive."

Her mother would've made her apologize again, for, as she

always said, no good apology contains an excuse for your ill behavior. But Delia smiled very graciously and apologized for the hurtful comment in her own turn, and then they cracked open the jug of milk and dipped in the cookies and had a glorious afternoon of it.

Delia shared all of the gossip that she'd been storing up for Mary, and that she'd hoped to tell yesterday. According to Mrs. Dennison, Camilla Wright (a very pretty, but snobbish girl in their year) had turned eighteen and no one had been sure that her destiny would come, but it had, first thing in the morning. But—she was quick to add after seeing the hurt on Mary's face—it was a dreadfully bad destiny.

Mrs. Dennison had said Camilla was to marry "that nincompoop, Augustus Primrose," and become the preacher's wife. To be fair to Delia, in her own eyes this was the worst destiny one could possibly receive. To have to marry someone as bland and prim as Augustus Primrose would have been a torture akin to no other.

If Grandma hadn't made the comment about Augustus being a "primpy little shrimp," Mary might have been in a bad way of things. But as it was, she was able to flutter away her hurt expression with only one rapid blink of the eyes.

"Imagine that," she said faintly, and Delia moved onto other topics, such as the fact that Tommy Edelstein—the same young man who had received his fortune on the toilet—had come down with the chicken pox even though almost no one over the age of eight years old ever got the pox, and that he'd had to be quarantined from his job at the post office.

Soon Mary was recovered enough to laugh genuinely at her stories, and they parted good friends once again. It wasn't long, however, before Augustus Primrose and his soon-to-be-bride were right back in the forefront of her mind.

The following market day, Grandma and Mary packed up the wagon with their prize vegetables and Mary pulled it down the hill and along High Street, to the village square where community gatherings were always held.

Mary was grateful that the wagon would be empty for the uphill walk home, because though she'd gained strength in her arms and shoulders it was still very heavy. Grandma walked behind to make sure that none of their bounty fell off on the rough road.

By the time they reached the square, sweat dripped into Mary's eyes, and she suddenly remembered how Camilla Wright had said that Mary's hair looked greasier than bacon in their fifth year. And now Augustus would marry Camilla instead of Mary. Camilla, whose deep auburn hair shone like autumn leaves in sunshine, and who was surely never greasy. Perhaps Augustus was exactly what Camilla needed, the impartial part of Mary reasoned. She'd give him flash, and he'd give her morality.

Nevertheless, she loosened her hair from its bun and tried to fluff it out at the roots so that it didn't look too bacon-y. Grandma watched this display with interest. It wasn't often that Mary showed concern about her looks.

"Here, dear," she said, and pushed a red rose from the small bundle they'd brought to sell behind her ear. It brought out the red tones in her hair in a very becoming way, and with her new pink dress she looked almost a different person than she had before her eighteenth birthday.

Mary, thinking that Grandma had noticed the grease as well, and that the flower helped hide it, submitted to the decoration without complaint. Otherwise, she never would've allowed such a frivolous display of vanity.

They were early to the market, but they weren't the only ones setting up. The Dennisons had a table of milk and cheese, their multitude of tow-headed children tumbling in the dust beneath it, and Simon had brought his best loaves—deep black pumpernickels and fragrant ryes and whole wheat studded with raisins. The smell of them wafting across the dusty lot made Mary's mouth water.

She and Grandma Isabella set up their table to its best display in the shade of a plum tree—they put the plumpest, reddest tomatoes in the front, and arranged the baskets of raspberries, strawberries and blueberries in tidy rows. The knobby squashes were corralled to the back, behind the kale and chard, because squash is an autumn food and not attractive in any season.

When Mary looked up next, a slight shock went through her when her gaze met with a pair of chestnut brown eyes. Theodore Primrose had arrived, and set up his table of meat and goat cheese and wild mushrooms across the square from them. He waved a friendly hello at Mary, and then went back to positioning a haunch of meat to its best advantage. He cut a handsome figure in the white apron he'd donned for the occasion: his waist narrow and his shoulders especially broad.

A minute or two past 8 a.m. the rest of the market vendors arrived. Dr. Hellman's boy set up his usual booth of tinctures and cures, Mr. Thomas laid out a form to sign up for shipments of his best alfalfa hay, and Mr. Bright brought trinkets and ribbons to sell.

The townsfolk turned out in force, dressed in their brightest colors and chatting gaily amongst themselves. Mary's parents even came, and bought up several of their squashes (Mary had confessed to them at her last visit that the squashes were their least purchased item), as well as their plumpest tomatoes.

Mrs. Hedelstein, the county judge, bought four baskets of raspberries and several bushels of chard, and they did a roaring trade with the church regulars—Pastor Primrose had recently mentioned in a sermon that garlic and onions could aid in purifying the soul.

Mary was too busy to notice, but their roses were bought up in the first hour, and soon young women all around the square wore roses tucked behind their ears, when only last week it had been the fashion to wear two spiraled braids behind the ears like fat cinnamon buns.

At the end of the dusty day the townsfolk left, trailing ribbons, and laden with meat, vegetables, and virtuous bottles of tinctures. As Grandma and Mary packed up, a shadow stepped in front of the sun. Mary squinted upward and her heart did a queer pitterpatter in her chest.

But where she was expecting to find Theodore, she instead found his younger brother. Augustus' wire-rimmed glasses flashed in the sun, and he sent a bland smile toward her. Grandma he ignored altogether, even though she stood solidly at Mary's side.

"Those were very pretty roses you sold today," he said, leaning over the table. "I wonder, do you have more of them at home? I'd love to purchase some for the parsonage. It isn't often we have fresh things to brighten it."

Was it Mary's imagination, or was he looking at her differently as he said it? Her heart beat faster. Perhaps Delia had misheard the rumor about Camilla marrying him, or had misunderstood. "Our rose bush is thick with them," she said, and glanced at Grandma. The old woman gave a resigned nod, and Mary continued. "We'd be happy to give you some. We only brought them along today as an afterthought."

"Mayhaps I'll stop by," he said, and with another bland smile, retreated across the square.

It took Mary a moment to gather herself before she could help Grandma reload the unsold vegetables into the cart and fold up the card table. Augustus had never spoken that way to her before, and the whole way home her imagination was caught up with images of the parsonage bedecked in roses, and herself sitting at the well-scrubbed wooden table, hands clasped with Augustus as they said their morning prayers.

It wasn't until they got home and Grandma spoke sharply to her about leaving the butter out on the table, that she came out of the daydreams and remembered that she was destiny-less, with no chance of marrying.

It was well and good to imagine herself a princess or heroine because there was no reality in those imaginings. But daydreaming about a life she'd never have hurt too much to bear.

For a few days after this incident she moped about the house, spending more time working on the last dress to be completed, the fine raspberry one, than walking out in the woods or brushing Rosie.

And then a distraction arrived in the form of Sunday dinner. Theodore had caught several striped bass out of the lake and asked for sorrel to garnish it. So once Mary had returned from church, and Grandma from delivering her vegetables, they set off into the woods to gather some.

Grandma showed her how to spy the miniature, heart shaped leaves in patches of sunlight, and picked a leaf for Mary to try right then and there. The flavor was sweet and lemony at the same time, like a burst of sunshine on the tongue.

They got so carried away picking that they ended up further from home than they'd intended. Grandma started to get tired—her eyes were dimmer than usual, and she'd had trouble spying the leaves among the other foliage in the forest floor.

When they were about a mile away she stumbled and nearly fell. Mary was so alarmed that she wanted to call a doctor—Grandma was as surefooted as a goat on most days—but Grandma only waved her away. Though she did let Mary offer an arm, and she leaned on it rather more than usual—even more than the time when they'd gone to church when Grandma didn't want to, and her hip had ached the whole way.

When they got home, she was too tired to wash the sorrel and mash the potatoes, so Mary settled her in the rocking chair while she did the washing and mashing. It was a great relief when Theodore arrived.

Within minutes, he had Grandma chuckling over a tale of Simon installing the outhouse too close to the well. "You should bring that boy along some time," she said, still cackling with mirth, though her knuckles were white where she clutched the rocker. "He'd do me some good."

"I'll bring him next week," Theo promised. And then he set to preparing the fish while Sparrow lounged on Grandma's feet.

After the Delia incident, Mary had forgotten most of her shyness around him. She certainly didn't understand him—and she couldn't think he was good—but she couldn't help but join in on their conversations with her own thoughts and observations.

Grandma seemed quite amazed when, during a discussion of flower gardens, Mary expressed a deep love for tulips. "There's something about their vividness," she said dreamily.

Theodore frowned. He'd grown up with the tulips in the window box of the parsonage. "I've never liked them much—

they're too obvious, too bland. Give me a woodflower any day over a tulip, with their subtle colors and layers and fantastic shapes. A flower like that can keep you gazing for hours." His eyes found Mary's then, and for a moment she felt confused, and almost mashed the sorrel instead of the potatoes.

Grandma was still tired when dinner was ready, so Mary pulled up the second rocking chair, and Theo sat with his back against the wall, his plate balanced on his knees.

All conversation was lost to the deliciousness of the food— the fish was buttery and lemony and sweet, the mashed potatoes so creamy and cloud-like, and their plates were so pretty with the delicate pink flesh of the fish dotted with green, heart shaped leaves, that the world narrowed to each bite. It wasn't until their plates were clean that they were able to think normally again.

Mary and Theodore cleaned up in companionable silence while Grandma rocked. By the time they finished she'd fallen asleep with her chin on her chest. Theodore gave her a worried glance, and whistled Sparrow up from her spot on a cushion.

"We'd best let her rest," he said, and gave Mary a crooked smile. "Goodnight, Miss Mary."

"Goodnight," she said, voice barely audible over the chirp of the crickets. In a twinkling he and his dog had disappeared into the dusk, the only hint of them Sparrow's bobbing white tail.

When the door had closed behind them, Grandma's eyes opened wide again. "You nearly gave me a heart attack, actually opening your mouth in front of Theodore Primrose!"

Mary looked up, startled for a moment, but then she saw that Grandma was teasing her and smiled. "He isn't so bad as they make him sound in town."

"I should think not. In fact, I'd go as far as to say he's quite a bit better."

Mary raised her eyebrows skeptically. She could feel a lecture in the works. "I thought you were tired," she said accusingly as Grandma drew a big breath to begin.

Grandma gave her a sharp look. "I'm not too tired for this. This is important. Now hush your mush and listen, child."

She waited until Mary had sat down in her rocker and laced her fingers primly in her lap. "Goodness is more complicated than our past mistakes and church habits and whether we're late to appointments, regardless of what this town would have you think. So many of the people who sit in pews every Sunday and spend all their energy trying not to curse when they stub their toes have never once done a bit of good for their hungry neighbors."

"Theodore is like me," she continued, after a long, shaky breath. "He finds God outside of church—in the wild places of the world. But he does more good than the whole congregation put together—bringing game to the poor on holidays so that they might have something jolly to eat, and passing his days with a lonely old lady, and he gets only dark rumors spread about him in thanks. Does that stop him?" She smacked an open palm against the wooden arm of her chair. "No!"

"I can't imagine his father is happy with his finding God outside of church," said Mary, thinking of how different he was from straight-laced Pastor Primrose.

"I'd imagine not. But his father respects his right to choose. The Primroses did one thing right with that boy—they raised him to be good first and to worry about what other people think second. It might have backfired on them in some respects, but it created a mighty fine human overall." At that

Grandma huffed. "Now, I'm very tired, and I'd like to go to sleep."

Mary helped her up out of her rocker and settled her in bed. But she didn't go up to her own bed right away. Instead she sat down beside the fire and stared into the orange flames, lost in thought about whether she had ever done any actual good in her entire life.

Chapter Nine

Mary wasn't worried about Grandma until the next day, when she didn't rise as usual to do the morning milking. Instead of being woken by a shout up the stairs, Rosie's urgent mooing blasted in through the window. She sat up to find the sun high in the sky.

Downstairs, Mary found the door to Grandma's room still shut tight, and so she pulled on her boots and trekked outside to milk Rosie. As soon as the cow's discomfort had been relieved, she strode down the trail and into town.

Dr. Hellman was in his office—a big-windowed room in the bottom of his house. Dusty bottles lined shelf after shelf, and a big black desk hovered menacingly in the middle of the room.

The doctor was pouring over a list of prescriptions and medications when she entered, his eyes magnified behind thick reading glasses.

Mary explained Grandma's symptoms, and he listened attentively, with many inquisitive "hmms" and thoughtful "mhmms," and then he packed up his big bag and draped his stethoscope around his neck to lead the charge back to Grandma's cottage.

She was sitting up in bed when they arrived, and looked relieved to see Mary, but vexed to see Dr. Hellman.

"I'm fine!" She insisted. "Right as rain." The glare she shot Mary was murderous. But Dr. Hellman convinced her to lie back for an exam regardless. "It doesn't hurt to check things out," he said in his kindly way. He listened at her chest, and took her pulse, and checked her reflexes.

Mary watched the proceedings with her own pulse thumping in her wrists, her fingernails dug into her palms with suspense.

"Your heart isn't as strong as it once was," he said at last. "You need to take things a bit slower, or you might wear it right out." Then he looked at Mary and pronounced her sentence: "Bed rest for three days, and then no strenuous activity for three weeks. You make sure she isn't pulling that cart of vegetables about, young lady."

Mary assured him that she'd keep Grandma quiet as could be, and would do her chores as well. She would've promised anything really, so long as Grandma was okay. Maybe even her destiny, if she'd had one to bargain with—though she didn't think that at the time.

So the following Sunday she rose at the crack of dawn, in order to both deliver the vegetables to the poor and attend church. She had expected to resent the task: it meant missing her breakfast with Delia, as well as her precious minutes of solitude and silence before the service started.

But instead she found that it in the quiet thank-yous of the people she delivered to and in their romping children with bare feet and the lean-hardworking look they all seemed to wear, there was something as good as, if not better than church.

She'd never done anything truly useful before for a stranger, and it gave her a sense of purposeful goodness—of selflessness and hard work for another's sake—that she'd never before felt sitting in a church pew.

The whole of her life she'd never really been needed, except perhaps last week when she'd gone to fetch the doctor, and now the sensation was positively uplifting.

She had expected the families to be embarrassed by the charity, but she soon found that while they might be poor in some ways, they were rich in others. Grandma had instructed her specifically before she set out that she was to take each family up on these offerings.

"It's a relationship," she explained, "and relationships have to go two ways." Several families invited her inside for conversation and a cup of strong, bitter coffee (she had to stop her nose wrinkling with every sip). Elderly Ms. Birdie even came out with two blueberry muffins fresh from the oven for them to warm their hands on.

They perched on the railings of the wagon while they nibbled on their muffins, and Ms. Birdie told her a story about how Grandma Isabella had once climbed the massive oak tree in her front yard to save a cat, and how the only thanks she'd received from the cat was a swat on the nose.

Mary loved to hear stories like these. They were very different than the ones the respectable set told about Grandma, and they reinforced what Mary herself thought about her relation—that she was brave and good, and that nothing earthly could stop her when she set out to do something.

When the 8 a.m. bell called everyone to church, she wheeled her wagon around and trudged through the dusty street. She parked the wagon outside—hidden in the bushes off to the side—and slunk in to sit in one of the farthest pews.

It was already late, and most of the congregation had gathered.

Church was better, somehow, than usual. The exercise of the morning had warmed her limbs, and she felt simultaneously alert and relaxed. Plus, all the kind things people had had to say that morning made it easier to weather the stares of the Moore cousins and the church ladies. Ms. Birdie even waved at her from a few pews over.

To make up for missing breakfast, she stopped by Delia's on her way home from church and invited her to Sunday dinner. It had been Grandma's idea, since Theodore had made good on his promise and invited Simon.

Theodore had three logs of creamy white goat cheese to share, and last night Mary had picked bag after bag of lettuce from the garden. Paired with sun-ripened tomatoes and peas fresh from the pod—and if Delia would consent to bring some —shaved walnuts from their backyard tree, it would be a scrumptious meal.

Delia agreed at once, particularly after she heard that Simon would be attending as well. The young baker was very mysterious, and had rarely been seen outside of the bakery since he turned eighteen. A whole host of rumors accompanied his every deed, and Theodore's funny stories about him— which Mary had repeated to Delia and Delia to the rest of town—had only heightened the town's fondness of him.

Mary felt very nervous leading up to the dinner. She washed the greens three times so that there was no grit, and fiddled with the soft green fabric of her gown until it lay just right, and was all around so bothered that Grandma couldn't help but grin into her knitting.

"What are you in a tizzy about?" she asked from her rocker.

"I'm worried that they all won't get along!" moaned Mary.

It had become exceedingly clear to her as soon as she'd gotten home that it had been a mistake to invite Delia. Delia had made her feelings about Theodore known, and while she now listened to Mary's stories about him without a negative word, it didn't mean she had changed how she felt.

But to Mary's relief, the dinner went off without a hitch. First Theo, Simon and Sparrow arrived: Theo with three fat rolls of goat cheese tucked in the crooks of his arms, Simon bearing a scrumptious apple and rhubarb pie with a top worked delicately into rose petals, and Sparrow wagging her beautiful banner of a tail.

Simon was still as sweet and shy and bumbling as he'd been as a child. He was fair where Theo was dark—his beard a deep auburn and his hair blonde from the sun, but he had the same brown eyes and long, thin nose that his brother did, and a very crooked, gallant smile. He was soft-spoken, and so exceedingly polite that it was impossible not to love him at once.

And then Delia arrived, stunning as always with her cloud of black curls pulled into a great globe upon her head, and air of dignity that she wore as well as her emerald-green cloak. A basket of walnuts swung from her arm, tucked in with a loaf of crusty bread. They settled themselves in a circle of blankets in the grass beneath the oak tree, Mary helping Grandma and her rocker outside.

Everyone made an exceptional effort to be charming and polite—Delia smiled her gleamingest smiles, Simon told them shyly about his recent work painting toadstools on a wedding cake, and Mary even got up the courage to share a story about the miller's son getting a bit of chalk stuck up his nose while his mother was picking out vegetables from the cart.

They'd had to launch a full-scale expedition to get the chalk out. Finally, Mr. Carnathan had whacked his son about the head in frustration, the boy had snorted in surprise and out the chalk had flown, leaving a white mark upon the road as it skittered away.

Theodore was rather quieter than usual—his main subject for stories being present—but he laughed often and ate with gusto, and glanced at Grandma frequently to see how she was faring. They all ate ravenously, because the food was fresh and fine, and none of them could bear wasting a bite of it. Even Grandma, whose usually ravenous appetite had been lessened, cleaned her plate and went back for seconds.

These expanded Sunday dinners soon became tradition. Simon was always happy for a chance to leave the society of his ill-built house, and Delia found that she rather enjoyed the merry friendship of the Primrose men, regardless of the rumors.

One evening as Mary walked her back home at dusk, she said thoughtfully, "I'd never have thought a man with a beard was handsome, but there's something so distinguished and manful about those Primrose boys. Especially Theodore, with the way his eyes crinkle when he smiles. If he hadn't shot that sweet little dog, I'd have thought him one of the most attractive men in town."

Mary herself had noticed that Theodore had exceptionally handsome eyes some time ago, but she kept the fact to herself, and only nodded along with her friend's musings.

The following Sunday, the dinners grew by yet another person. Mary had taken the cart out early again that morning, and as she'd walked she met with Mrs. Alice Hedelstein, a kindly woman in her sixties with short grey hair and dreamy, hazel eyes.

"Good morning Judge," said Mary politely—Alice Hedelstein was the judge for the whole county, and she often traveled out of Tolling Bell to hear cases.

"Morning Mary," said Mrs. Hedelstein. She had purple circles under her eyes, and her white hair stuck up in the back. Mary wondered if she'd just gotten back into town after a case.

"What have you got this morning?" Mrs. Hedelstein was one of the richest citizens of Tolling Bell, and the vegetables were for the poorest—they sold only the leftovers at market—but she was so nice that Mary stopped her cart and let her have a look.

"Do you have anything in particular in mind for your Sunday dinner?" Mary asked.

Mrs. Hedelstein held up a tomato. "Why, no. It's just me most Sundays, ever since Sadie passed last fall." There was a wistfulness to her tone that was unusual for the keen-eyed judge.

Mary nodded soberly, remembering Mrs. Hedelstein's lively wife. She'd had the ruddiest cheeks of anyone Mary had ever met, and the brightest black eyes. "You know," she began tentatively, not sure if she was being proper, but quite sure that she was being good, "Grandma and I host a Sunday dinner every week. You'd be welcome to come along if you'd like."

"Oh!" said the judge, seeming taken aback by the invitation, and looking at boring Mary Ellmire in a different light. "That'd be just the thing! What time do you all show?"

"People trickle in as they please," Mary said truthfully, but knowing that Mrs. Hedelstein was a very punctual kind of person she added, "You'd be safe to arrive at five o' clock."

"I'll see you then," Mrs. Hedelstein said, and they parted, both feeling very pleased.

When Mary got home, she found Grandma up and about, already working on a giant meat pie stuffed with venison and mashed potatoes.

"I hope it's alright, but I've invited Judge Hedelstein to join us tonight." She took up scrubbing the potatoes, and didn't meet Grandma's eye—she felt suddenly anxious. An unexpected guest to dinner was just the sort of thing that would've thrown her mother into a tizzy. "She said she was on her own most Sundays."

Grandma laid a hand on her arm. "That's wonderful dear. We'll have a real party of it." As they waited for the guests to show, Mary was very nervous again, and almost had her meager old appetite back. "Oh, why have I been so nervous these past two Sundays!" she lamented aloud.

Grandma looked up from her knitting. "It's a good thing. It means that you're taking risks and opening your world up to others. It isn't easy doing that, but it's very character building."

She'd said just the right thing. In that perspective, Mary's nerves weren't the flutters of a timid soul too scared to face the world. They were a sign that she was growing, and trying new things. It is hard not to feel hungry when you're doing that.

So when Theodore, Simon and Sparrow arrived, she greeted them even more cheerfully than she had last week, and sampled the goose popovers Theodore had constructed to go along with the pie without fear of a bellyache later.

Simon had again brought dessert, this time a great confectionary delight of lemon meringue piled with clouds of whipped cream and candied lemon peel. It quivered with every step he took, and he had to carefully ease it onto the already full counter so as not to disrupt the whipped cream.

Sparrow brought a pinecone, which at first they laughed at, but then found that it made a perfect centerpiece—it accented the pie and meringue perfectly.

Mrs. Hedelstein was next to arrive, a dusty bottle under her arm which she soon revealed to be a very old, very fine bottle of port that she'd been saving for a special occasion. Grandma especially looked delighted at this, and gave the woman a kiss on the cheek.

As usual Delia was last on the scene, but she made up for it with a platter of roast squash drizzled with honey and shaved nuts, and sprigged with fresh rosemary.

At first the old group felt uncomfortable sitting down to dinner on the grass with such an esteemed personage as Judge Hedelstein. But she plunked herself down with spryness surprising for one in her sixties, and looked so very at home and pleased with the arrangement that they didn't have a second thought about it.

"Call me Alice," she said after Simon had stumbled over her title for the third time that evening. "This isn't a courtroom, and am I ever glad it isn't!"

After that she felt like one of the group completely. It helped that she found Simon's poor building skills hilarious—she spent a good twenty minutes grilling him about the ways the old cottage was slowly collapsing around him, and laughing uproariously as he confirmed the rumors that had been going around town.

"Perhaps," she had begun after he retold the tale of the raccoon family moving into the outhouse, "You ought to stick to meringues. If you'd like I'll come out and take a look at things for you. I've always suspected my destiny got it wrong, and I should've been a builder."

They worked their way through the sumptuous piles of food with glasses of deep, rich port that set their tongues dancing, until they got to what was considered the crowning achievement: the lemon meringue.

Mary had often felt that dessert was missing from Sunday dinner, and Simon had so creatively and deliciously filled the gap that she couldn't keep her mind off that meringue all through the meal.

At last it was lowered carefully into the grass, and great slices of quivering lemon and cream were cut and slid onto each plate. Mary took a bite and closed her eyes at the sheer explosion of flavor—it was tart and sweet and creamy and light all in one, and the candied lemon peel added texture to the occasional bite. She ate up her entire piece and wished she could have more despite the bursting seams of her stomach.

That evening Mary went up to bed full and happy and still flushed with laughter from the evening. It wasn't until she got to the top of the stairs that she realized her bed was still unmade from the prior night—the covers rumpled, the pillow tossed to the floor. She'd been in such a hurry to milk Rosie and dash off to deliver the vegetables before church, that she had plum forgotten to do it.

She chuckled. It was a hearty little chuckle, very different from the girlish giggles she had restricted herself to before her eighteenth birthday. How much she had changed. She lay with her head sinking into her newly retrieved pillow, her hair fanning out around her, and thought that if only she'd had a destiny, she'd have been perfectly happy.

Chapter Ten

Dr. Hellman gave Grandma the okay to resume her normal activities the next week, and soon Grandma was out milking the cow in the mornings and accompanying Mary while she delivered the vegetables—though Mary insisted on pulling the wagon.

They were both mightily relieved: Grandma had been feeling as though she might explode if she wasn't able to use her body soon, and Mary realized how very lonely she had been doing all the outdoor chores on her own.

She remembered back to the old days, when she used to sit in her room for hours all by herself, working on her needlepoint until her stitches were so small they almost seemed to disappear. That those stitches had been the pride of her life made Mary incredulous.

These days she had so many better things to be proud of: her braveness in making friends with people who intimidated her—her work growing and delivering the very best vegetables in the town for the very poorest people—her labor on the farm each day so that things were easier for Grandma.

That wasn't to say that she didn't still love to sit down and sew out a beautiful scene on a rainy afternoon. But it was no longer the centerpiece of her life. And her sewing, it seemed, had flourished despite her neglect.

Before she'd sewn the scenes and patterns she found in her sewing books, and so her stitching—while very fine—was the same as many works before it. But lately she found herself sewing things she had seen during the day: a pattern of rain-drops falling from the roof eaves as a border on a curtain, or a mossy glen she'd stumbled upon during her walks, the indi-vidual stalks of moss lit by the sun so that they looked like a green velvet dress laid out on the forest floor.

One Sunday, Alice spotted one of Mary's half-finished patterns—this one of the miniature jugs of cream and bundles of cheese and wheels of butter in various sizes from the cave shelving—and was so delighted with it that she asked Mary whether she could pay her to embroider a similar pattern on her kitchen linens.

Mary was so thrilled that she did a dance that evening before bed, milk jugs and cheese wheels made of thread leaping and pivoting in her imagination. She set to it the very next day—though some of her other chores, such as weeding the garden and doing the evening milking—occasionally called her away and made it slower going than it would have been usually.

Mary applied herself with good-hearted dedication to the embroidery. She raced into the house between chores to pick up her needle and hoop, woke early and sat in the window— for the best light—hunkered over her thin scraps of fabric as she tested the trickier parts of the design.

Grandma was bored by all the sewing. "You hardly pay attention to me at all anymore," she'd moan from her rocking chair as Mary started on the fifth dishcloth. "Don't you think about anything but sewing?"

And Mary would muster all of her willpower and set the work aside for a half hour of being needled by Grandma that the only reason she'd stopped working was out of guilt, and how she clearly didn't love her grandmother at all.

Those laments would have horrified Mary if she hadn't recognized the curl of a smile on Grandma's lip. "Don't tease me, you old witch," she finally said after an entire day of being needled. "You know I love you more than I ever imagined I could love anything."

Grandma couldn't even try to hide her smile after that.

When at last Mary had finished her last dishcloth and had delivered the small bundle (so little for all that work!) to Alice's house, Alice paid her handsomely for the linens, and told her they'd be the pride of the kitchen. Privately, she also determined to bring them to the next church banquet, because she felt that when the rest of Tolling Bell saw them they'd soon be knocking on Mary's door.

Now that Mary was no longer occupied by sewing, she and Grandma began to plan another adventure out into the woods.

Grandma had been itching to get out again, especially with the season of fine warm weather fully upon them. Various projects were suggested: a venture into the lower glens to look for any leftover fiddlehead ferns, a trip into the foothills of the mountains to pick wildflowers, an expedition to look for tea leaves.

It was Theodore who finally settled it for them. "You know what I've been thirsting for lately?" he said one warm afternoon after he'd helped Mary shovel out the cow shed.

"What'd he say?" called Grandma from where she was perched fragilely on the fence. The wind was hot and loud in her old ears, and she hated to be left out of anything.

"I was going to say," said Theodore, raising his voice so

that she could hear, "that I've been dying for a sip of root beer."

Mary had only had root beer once, when her father had brought some specially for her mother's birthday. She remembered it being syrupy and crisp at the same time. She swallowed hard, suddenly very thirsty.

Grandma lowered herself from the fence with a small groan. "I haven't had root beer for a decade at least."

After that, neither Grandma nor Mary could get the phantom taste off the back of their tongues. And so one afternoon, after the garden had been tended to, they set out to look for sassafras root to brew their very own root beer.

It felt good to be out with Grandma again—to have her point out the types of birds and their identifying characteristics, and to explain how lichen formed and why streams babbled. They finally found a sassafras tree in the open canopied woods that blanketed the mountain side.

Grandma showed Mary how to recognize the three-lobed leaves, and then she handed over the spade and set her granddaughter to digging while she rested against the trunk. After a half an hour's hard digging through the packed soil, Mary hacked up some dirty orange roots. They rinsed them off in the nearby stream and set off back toward home, Grandma leaning on Mary's arm.

She didn't seem quite as tired as last time, but still, Mary wondered if mayhaps their expeditions were too much for her these days. When they got home Mary tucked her into her favorite rocker, and set to whipping up a dinner of thin-sliced summer squash and crispy, buttery eggs—cooked the way Grandma liked them best, so that the yolk dribbled out and set the squash swimming.

"We'll work on the root beer tomorrow," she promised, tucking the roots into the pantry. "Tonight you ought to rest."

Grandma took her hand in thanks, and the frailness of her grip frightened Mary more than even her tiredness three weeks before. Grandma Isabella, seeing the fear, only smiled. "Don't worry, Mary. It isn't my time just yet, and even if it was, I have lived a full and glorious life."

Her granddaughter kissed her wrinkled cheek and settled herself in the rocker with a cookbook and an old quilt. Grandma watched her for a few long minutes.

"You ought to ask Theodore to borrow a novel. You'll enjoy it more than one of these fussy old cookbooks."

Mary looked up, surprised. "I thought you didn't approve of novels," she said, remembering the days when she'd been a young girl who'd always wanted to go the library to hear the picture books read aloud, and Grandma had chastised her that it was no good living outside of the present, and that novels were escapes from reality for the weak minded.

Grandma shrugged. "Even old dogs can learn new tricks. He lent me one last winter that was simply marvelous—with true love and fighting and great escapes through the mountains."

Mary smiled. "Well, perhaps I will then."

When she woke the next day to the cow mooing, Mary knew that Grandma had been tireder than she'd let on the day before. She milked Rosie with urgent, worried fingers, and then raced off for the doctor, the chickens clucking indignantly that they hadn't been fed at her retreating form.

As soon as Dr. Hellman was at Grandma's side, giving her a full examination, Mary set off again. This time she followed the stream up to the lake, and was in such a great hurry that she didn't even hear Sparrow's "roo roo!"

She jogged up the steps, tears of fear and worry in her eyes and knocked impatiently on Theo's door. It swung open before her hand could leave the wood, and there was Theo, his shirt rather unbuttoned at the collar, a book clutched in his hand with the place kept by a careful finger. He took in Mary's fear-stricken appearance in a glance and pulled her right in through the door.

"What's happened?" he asked urgently. "Where's Grandma?"

"She's ill again," Mary said, her voice quivering. "I've just got the doctor there, but last time was so awful waiting all by myself, and last night Grandma was saying how she borrowed a novel from you, and it made her very happy, so I thought if she was stuck in bed again—"

Theodore didn't ask why she hadn't left this very non-urgent matter for after the doctor had left, but instead pulled several well-worn novels from his shelf, whistled Sparrow off her divan by the window, and grabbed Mary's small hand in his own large, callused one so that she didn't get left in the wake of his long strides.

In any other instance Mary would have protested mightily to hand holding—especially with someone as disreputable as Theodore Primrose—but to her surprise, she found his firm grip to be comforting. She trotted along at his side, and told him about their adventure yesterday, and how Grandma had seemed tired afterwards but not so tired as last time, and how she'd known as soon as the cow wasn't milked that she must've been hiding it all along.

The doctor had just finished examining her when they burst in the front door, his thin mouth even thinner than usual with the news he had to tell. He sat down in the rocker, and Sparrow rested her head on his white-jacketed lap.

"Your grandmother's heart is beating faster than it ought," he said in his grimmest tone, "and she needs to be very careful with her activity level, or she might bring on an attack."

Mary's eyes welled up with tears at this news, but

Theodore gripped her hand fiercely and together they bore it out. When Dr. Hellman had gone and Grandma had been set up in her bed with Theo's favorite adventure novel and a large glass of sweet, cold water from the brook, they sat out on the paddock fence together so that they could talk without disturbing her.

Mary was on her way to believing that Theodore Primrose was one of the dearest souls on the planet, but there was one matter that still had yet to be cleared up.

"Theo," she said after a long minute of gathering her courage, the heels of her boots dangling against the fence post. "Why did you shoot Sparrow's leg off?"

Theo looked down at where his little dog had curled in a ball in the long grass, her silky fur mingling with the wheat stalks. "That one act has haunted me more than anything I've ever done," he said, and looking at the twist of his lips, Mary knew it was true. "Are you sure you want to know? I'm afraid you'll think worse of me."

"I'd like to know, if you don't mind telling..." she said, bashful over her curiosity.

He sighed, pressed his fingers to his temples, and began his story.

"When I first moved out to the cabin on the lake I kept chickens. Not meat chickens, but layers. My mother had given me chicks to start my brood with shortly before she passed away, and I raised them up by hand. They were brilliant chickens—bright russet red and smarter than some folks in the village. Each knew her name, and would fly up onto my shoulder when I called. I got real attached to them, living out there on my lonesome."

Mary closed her eyes against the warm sunshine—she could just picture Theo with chickens on his shoulders, strutting around the small yard of his cabin.

"One afternoon, I was on my way home from a hunt and I heard a ruckus in the coop. The sun was just setting over the mountains, and I remember running up the hill, the sunlight half blinding me, squinting to see what was happening. Before my very eyes, a red animal pounced on my nearest and dearest friend, Bertha, and ripped her to smithereens. So I started hollering and running, my blood boiling, and the animal—it looked like a fox with its white-tipped tail—took off running. It was a bad shot. I couldn't see with the glare, and it was too far, but I was furious and my chickens were dead, and I took it anyway."

"I could tell right off it hadn't hit the way it should have—and immediately I regretted acting so rashly, for no animal should have to die in so much pain—so I followed the fox into the woods to take it out of its misery. When I found it, I realized that it wasn't a fox after all, but a little red and white dog. Her ribs stuck up stark against her fur, and those big, liquid brown eyes looked up at me with such kindness and trust, even after what I had done to her... Well, I scooped her up and ran with her into town. Doctor Hellman said that the only way to save her was to take the leg off, but that he'd had a hunting dog who lost a leg in a trap, and he'd done just fine and likely she would too."

Theo stared off into the woods, his words lost to thought. The light was thick and red, and pollen and dandelion seeds floated on the lazy breeze. This close, Mary could see the individual bristles of Theo's beard, and his thick, dark eyelashes. He really was very handsome, once you got beyond the beard.

"I brought her home after the surgery, and fed her a few good meals, and she's been the jolliest little dog I could ever have imagined. We both learned things, I expect. She's never attacked another chicken, and I've never again shot without being sure of myself first."

"Thank you for telling me that," Mary said, when he'd finally met her eyes again. "The people in town tell all sorts of tales, and I had always wondered about the truth."

Theodore bowed his head. "I've heard the rumors myself, and while they certainly exaggerate things, I never felt comfortable correcting people. I did shoot Sparrow in a moment of temper, and I deserve to be reviled for it."

Mary frowned, thinking back on the first time she'd ever seen Sparrow's missing leg. "Do you remember the first time you stopped by here, when I was brushing Rosie?"

Theodore's somber face lightened. "I remember how you ducked behind her, and I thought you were the strangest person I'd ever spoken to."

"Well we're even then, for I thought you were the most terrifying creature I'd ever laid eyes on. I'm sorry I judged you so quickly."

They smiled at each other, and Mary knew then that they'd be the dearest friends for the rest of their lives, because the gateway to deep friendship is admitting honestly what you initially thought of each other.

Chapter Eleven

WHILE GRANDMA WAS BEDRIDDEN, Mary was busier than ever. It now fell on her to milk the cow, deliver the vegetables, wash the dishes and make the meals. On top of that she had mending to do for her winter clothes, and so often she was up until late in the night bent over a candle and wishing she hadn't misplaced her sewing glasses—her eyes easily became strained in the dim light.

She also had started the root beer—chopping the sassafras root along with sugar and other herbs and berries, stirring them over the stove until sweat dripped down her back and the liquid darkened to a pleasing red-brown color. When it had cooled, she added yeast to it, divvied it into glass bottles, and sealed them shut. After a few days of fermentation, they'd be ready to drink. And she'd be... well, she'd be damned if Grandma died without a taste of the stuff.

On fine afternoons Grandma would send Mary outside to dip her toes in the stream or explore the cool, shady woods outside the cabin. She always sent her out with a fabricated task to do—to gather flowers from the garden to brighten the kitchen or collect flat stones from the stream to line the walkway with.

But Mary knew that Grandma was only looking out for her sanity, and she was grateful for these excursions. She needed them to decompress—to let her thoughts slide fluidly through her head instead of getting snagged in tangles of worry and fear for the future—she felt terribly weighed down by worry for Grandma, and housework left too much time to dwell on it.

The one good thing about Grandma's bedrest was that it gave them extra time together. It started with Grandma needing her to fetch things for her—it is hard to keep any distance from the person who fetches and cleans your bedpan, which can be a curse or a blessing depending on the person.

If anything, she and Grandma felt more like equals now. When Grandma was trapped in bed she could not storm or rage the same as she could on her own two feet—and Mary was able to stomp her feet and scold her right back. Soon, she could even do it without tears coming to her eyes.

Once, after Grandma had gone into a particular rage—this one because her feet were too cold and Mary couldn't seem to plump the pillow properly—Mary had perched tentatively on the end of the bed. "I envy you, you know," she said frankly.

That snapped the old woman right out of her surliness. "What do you mean?"

"You're so honest about how you feel all of the time, regardless of how it makes other people feel."

Grandma Isabella eyed her suspiciously. "That doesn't sound like a compliment."

"Maybe not," Mary said. "But it must be incredibly freeing."

At that the old woman smiled. "It is freeing. After a lifetime of worrying about everyone else—of tiptoeing around egos and follies and flaws—it is a great comfort to kvetch when you want to kvetch."

After that Grandma had fewer rages and Mary sat on the edge of Grandma's bed more often. They had long conversations about their lives before the cabin and Grandma told her about the olden days, before the railway had come to Tolling Bell and made the bigger cities accessible.

On one unseasonably cold afternoon, when a great thunderstorm whipped up a frenzy of chill mountain wind so that the oak tree's branches tapped and scraped at the window above Grandma's bed, Mary climbed right into bed with Grandma. They pulled the blankets up to cover their legs, and Grandma's fingers deftly knitted away at a bright red scarf.

"Grandma," Mary began after a long silence, filled only by the crackle of the fire in the fireplace. "What was it like when you got your destiny?" It was only lately, as she'd begun to find shoots of happiness in her new life even without a destiny, that she'd been able to ponder this question.

Grandma patted Mary's hand. Her old, wrinkled skin felt cool, and very soft to the touch. Mary could feel the knobs of her knuckles underneath—it reminded her of the feeling of holding a chicken—all feathers and bone.

"It's funny you ask—I was just thinking that this weather reminds me mightily of that day. Only it was January, and we were in the middle of a raging blizzard. I was so worried that my bird wouldn't be able to find me, that it might get lost in the snow, or that it wouldn't be able to find its way into the house—the only opening we could afford with all that wind and snow was the tiniest crack in my bedroom window. But it came, right around supper time. Only it didn't come in through the window—we had just sat down around the table when there was a great billow of smoke, and it puffed right out through the fireplace! Its wings were soot-streaked, and its eyes were half closed with exhaustion after the journey. It dropped my scroll in my lap, and then landed clumsily on the table and rested for a while, before pecking at my toast and flying back on up the chimney."

Grandma paused to measure her scarf against her arm, and then kept knitting. Once the stitches were flowing steadily, she started up talking again. "I was completely shocked by the destiny itself—I'd grown up an only child, and the idea of being around children all day seemed almost unbearable. And it took me a while to come around to the idea of marrying your grandfather." She smiled wistfully. "So many people get destinies and they hardly know the person they're supposed to marry. But I'd grown up with Byron Ellmire as my closest companion. We were best friends, and I couldn't imagine ever thinking of him as anything more than like a brother."

"I didn't know that," Mary said eagerly. "How'd you come around to the idea?"

Grandma laughed, remembering. "Well, I made a bit of a mess of it, to be honest. I refused to tell him that my destiny had singled him out as the one. He was almost six months younger than me, and so for six whole months, I walked around all haughty, learning my new trade as headmistress and ignoring him. But then he got *his* destiny, and instead of being clear about who he ought to marry, it was terribly vague. I think it said something like *Marry a woman in charge*, and so he went gallivanting off, trying to find his woman in charge. He was a real catch back then, green-eyed and handsome, and so there was veritable flock of girls who were more than happy to take charge of him. He picked out the bossiest, prettiest one, Mary Beth Chook, and I thought I was going to die of jealousy, watching them flit around town together. But I was too stubborn to say anything, even though my own feelings had changed dramatically since I'd first received my destiny. I felt that if I wasn't his first choice, then he didn't deserve me, and I was fixing to spend the rest of my days alone."

"It took another six months before we finally got things sorted out. Mary Beth had started hinting for a ring, see. And your grandfather was feeling uneasy about that. Finally, he cornered me at the schoolhouse during my lunch while the children played at recess and pulled me aside. 'Mary Beth wants me to propose,' he said—and I'll always remember how dead silent the children went, listening to every word. 'But before I do that, I just have to be certain. Isabella, I have to be honest with you—I've always thought you were the one for me, and I've missed you terribly these last few months.'"

"Well, after that, I had to tell him the truth. At first I was afraid that he'd be terribly angry with me for muddling everything up the way I had, but he just threw his head back and roared with laughter in that way he used to do—at such a decibel that it hurt my ears. We got married only a few weeks later, in a small ceremony by the lake. Mary Beth never forgave me."

Mary laughed. Mary Beth Chook had eventually become Mary Beth Moore, Mary's great aunt, when she'd married her mother's uncle. "I suppose it all worked out in the end."

"It did indeed," said Grandma, and she put down her knitting. "Now shoo, I need a nap after all that talking."

ON GRANDMA'S weak days and Mary's sad days, she sometimes felt as though she was getting to love Grandma so dearly only so she would lose her and break her heart. If Grandma had known these thoughts, she would have cackled and told her to hold on for a wild ride, because that was life in a nutshell. Loss is inevitable whenever you love someone or something dearly enough. And why bother living at all, if you don't have anything you love?

But Mary never did tell Grandma, and so she was left to have hard days of missing her grandmother before she'd gone, and good days of loving her so ferociously that she couldn't imagine losing her.

Sunday dinners had become difficult since Grandma's bed sentence. She became irritable when they all gathered in the kitchen—she felt left out from the festivities, and she'd often say that if she was miserable, they ought to be as well. But they just laughed until she could laugh at herself, and soon everyone was jolly again.

Mostly they crowded around her bed to eat, so that she didn't feel so out of things as she might otherwise. The scene reminded Mary of a group of courtiers gathered around their queen, vying with each other to earn a smile or laugh. Theodore and Simon kept up an act of constant humor— ragging on each other mercilessly and telling tall tales from their childhood.

Alice always had some difficult case for the group to chew on, though she kept the names of the people involved anony- mous—it was a small town, and rumor spread fast enough as it was. Mary was particularly good at picking out the lines of right and wrong in each case. Delia attributed it to the "fine- tuned sense of propriety" she'd spent her life developing.

"You know, Mary," said Alice one evening. "If you weren't so busy already, I'd say you should be a judge. You have such a clear idea of justice."

"Yes," said Grandma wryly. "She could make a robin feel guilty for pecking worms on rainy days. She'd say it was an unfair advantage."

Mary laughed with the rest of the group, but quietly hugged the compliment to herself. It felt very nice to be good at something aside from needlework or mending fences for once. That night as she went to bed it repeated in her mind, like a happy parade, until finally she fell asleep and dreamt of robins on rainy days.

It had now been four months since Mary had come to live with Grandma, and while she had mostly settled into the rhythm of her new life, there was still the occasional surprise. One night she was out tucking Rosie in when a howl from the surrounding woods filled the air. The sound was so eerie that it made the hair stand up on her arms.

"Wolves!" she gasped as she ran inside, shuddering. "Where should I hide Rosie?!"

Grandma only laughed at her. "Wolves wouldn't bother a big healthy cow like Rosie—and anyway, those are loons, not wolves, you goose."

Other wildlife besides the loons came in to the land surrounding the cottage. Deer could be seen grazing the long grasses alongside the path to town in the early mornings, and Mary once spied a lumbering black bear through the trees on her way to collect butter from the cave. Owls frequently called back and forth across the clearing the house was in, though she was never out late enough to see one, and song-birds abounded in the tree canopies. As she became comfortable with these new types of neighbors, she grew to enjoy and look out for them like they were old friends, though she was very sure she never wanted to meet a black bear face to face.

As far as their human neighbor went, it was hard for Mary to remember how she had ever been scared of him. In fact, she was beginning to feel something entirely different—something as furtive and shy as the vole that lived under the fallen fence post next to the shed.

When the root beer was ready, she pinned a note to his door:

Theo,

Stop by the cottage for a special refreshment this afternoon. Grandma wanted to thank you for the idea.

-Mary

The whole rest of the day Mary felt fidgety. As she harvested blueberries in the garden she kept her gaze trained on the path that led up to the lake, waiting for a certain broad shouldered form to come down it.

Noon passed, and he didn't show. She'd been dawdling in the garden, hoping to catch first evidence that he was on his way, and her neck was sunburnt, her arms tired. She stood to give up and go inside when her eyes caught motion through the trees. At first she thought it was just a glimmer on the water, but then a shifting shadow drew her gaze.

He blended into the trees so well that she had to squint to make out his form. As he got closer, she saw the green plaid shirt that had rendered him invisible, and his gun slung on a leather strap over his shoulder.

"One thirsty hunter, at your service," he called once he got within earshot.

Mary's stomach did a funny leap—like a new calf on the first fine spring day. It was suddenly hard to look directly at him, like looking into the noon sun above.

They fell into step as they walked into the cottage. Grandma sat in her rocker, eyes narrowed against the brilliance of the light in the doorframe. "Come for your refreshments, eh?" she crowed at Theodore.

Mary's laugh came out very high and breathy. Grandma cast a shrewd glance at her, and hefted herself up from the rocker with great effort. "Let's have a taste of it then."

They gathered around the squat kitchen table, and Mary produced the stoppered bottle of root beer. It was dark brown, and when she uncapped the stopper, a sweet hiss of air escaped.

"It smells like root beer," said Theodore encouragingly, peering into the thin mouth of the bottle. As Mary poured the concoction into their glasses, a thick foam rose up from the liquid. Grandma nodded her approval.

"Shall we make a toast?" she asked, gripping her glass in one white-knuckled hand.

Theodore considered. "To friendship and the earth's good providence," he said at last, and lifted the glass into the air. They clinked their glasses, and Mary took a sip.

The foam coated her upper lip and tickled her nose—an odd sensation—but the root beer itself was sweet and cold and medicinal. The perfect antidote to the muggy day outside. She felt now that she was glad she had worked in the garden today, because the sweat and the heat of it had made that first sip even sweeter.

Grandma closed her eyes as she sipped, swaying slightly, as though to recall her own days of drinking root beer under a hot breeze after an afternoon of work. Theodore drained half his glass, and smiled at them from under a mustache of white foam.

"Tastes just as it ought," he declared. "I'm only jealous you didn't invite me along for the adventure of gathering the ingredients."

They spent the afternoon sipping in quiet satisfaction.

When there were only traces of foam at the bottom of the jug, Theodore rose and stretched his arms above his head. "I'd better be off. I've got my own housework to do yet, and I was hoping to fit in some mending."

Mary waited until Sparrow's tail had disappeared out the door, and then went out to sit on the paddock fence, where she could surreptitiously watch Theo's back as it disappeared into the trees.

For the first time, her imagination followed him home. She wondered what he was doing now, and if he ever wondered about her.

She pictured him sweeping the floor of his little cabin—surely he would use long, steady strokes, patience in every movement. And sitting on the front steps of his house, needle in hand as he mended a sock. There was something about the image that made her chest ache with tenderness.

If she were his wife, she wouldn't take the needle from him in that clucking, bustling way she'd seen other women do. She'd sit quietly at his side, and revel in every stitch. If she were his wife...

Her cheeks flushed. She jumped down from the fence and went to fetch a leaf of hay for Rosie.

Chapter Twelve

To DISTRACT herself from these new, unwelcome thoughts about Theo, she'd thrown herself into her chores with new gusto—wiping down the cabin surfaces until they shone in a muted, well-oiled way, baking new bread recipes that were sometimes inedible and other times utterly divine, and trying to fulfill Grandma's every passing whim and longing.

When Grandma mentioned that she'd noticed the wild grapes on vine that grew up outside of her window were fully ripe and that they made the best jam—with only the smallest hint of desire in her voice—Mary marched right outside with a basket and picked every last one of them.

"You shout instructions, and I'll be your hands," she told Grandma as she hauled them onto the counter.

So Grandma directed her as she rinsed the fruit and set it into the great copper pot, heated several heaping cups of sugar in it, and then mashed the grapes into a thick, purple paste. Soon it was burbling merrily away on the stovetop. Mary felt soothed as she stood and stirred it, as though she could settle her mind in the cozy warmth of the pot. After a spell,

Grandma directed her to squeeze in lemon juice. Then it was more stirring, until at last the jam was ready to be ladled into the hungry mouths of waiting jars.

When the jam had cooled, Mary heated two slices of one of her more successful bread experiments on the woodstove until they were golden-brown and crispy, slathered them with butter, and spooned on two heaping tablespoons of jam.

Grandma had been right: the grapes made divine jam. It tasted like sunshine and woods and wild summer rains—grapey and sweet and tangy. They ate a whole jar between themselves that very day, and then tucked another three into the pantry to save for winter.

They decided that they'd set the last two aside to bring to market, so Mary tucked them in with her heaping load of vegetables, regretting with every step in front of the wagon that she'd have to part with them. However, there were other, more agreeable reasons to go to market.

She had seen Augustus Primrose at the market again that Thursday prior, and while he hadn't ever come over to pick roses from their bushes, he seemed quite delighted to see her, bought up their entire stock of broccoli, and had even brushed a stray lock of hair behind her ear—which brought a brilliant flush to her cheeks.

He was also very much unmarried.

Camilla had married a preacher's son from the next village over, and Delia's rumors had turned out to be false. This gave Mary an odd, mixed up feeling inside—she felt that she ought to be happy, more than she actually was happy. It is a difficult thing when we outgrow our fantasies, only to find them finally within reach.

That evening as she sat at her grandmother's bedside and told her about the day, Grandma sighed. "It sounds like you just may get your wish of marrying that terrible Augustus Primrose." She said it sourly, but Mary blushed—for Grandma Isabella tended to be very wise about these things. And, she reasoned, any husband would be better than no husband at all, wouldn't it?

It was late August now, and Delia's eighteenth birthday was drawing near. As luck would have it, it happened to fall on a Sunday. The whole Sunday dinner group was very excited—Simon had planned a masterpiece of a cake, Theodore had shot a turkey for them to roast, and Alice had already brought her finest plum wine up from the cellar. They planned to carry Grandma out on her mattress so that she might join in the fun too, without having to exert a hair on her head.

Mary was the only one with reservations, which was understandable given her destinyless state. She was trying to be a good sport about it, but the idea of listening to them all gush over the new life Delia was to lead made her feel rather sick inside.

When Sunday rolled around, Mary was still feeling so very mixed up about Augustus Primrose, and worried about Grandma—and the whole time she couldn't keep Theodore off of her mind—that she was wholly unprepared to act jolly and normal for Delia's sake.

She relived her own terrible last birthday as she towed the empty vegetable cart home. Remembering how very still she had held herself, and what great hopes she had held shot her heart through with pity—and she shed several tears into the dusty road as she walked.

The rest of the day was too busy for self-pity. She had sweet potatoes to roast and a salad to toss and bread to bake. She was so absorbed in her preparations that she was quite taken aback by the knock at the door, a good hour before guests usually arrived.

She opened it to find Delia, simply glowing with grown up beauty. With one glance at her face, Mary knew for certain that her destiny had come. Her friend had never looked so beautiful. Her hair was a tight cascade of curls around her delicate shoulders, her skin glowed deep brown with golden undertones, and her gold gown set off her black eyes magnificently.

Mary herself had prepared specially for the big day—she wore her raspberry chiffon, and had brushed her hair until it shone like silk, but compared to this magnificent creature she felt like a girl playing dress up.

"Shall we go for a walk?" Mary asked, thinking that she might need some sunshine to help soften the blow. It must be a glorious destiny for Delia to look like that.

They went out into the pines, and walked lazily through the motes of sunshine pouring down through the trees.

"So," said Mary at last, looking up at her friend with what she hoped was a purely loving and excited expression.

"It came this morning at breakfast. And it was so soft and gentle—its wings brushed my cheeks as it flew away. And Mary! I was so excited I wanted to run over and tell you immediately, but mother and father insisted I stay through supper at least."

"What did it say?" Mary asked, suddenly impatient for the news to come and be done already.

"Why, it told me that I'd marry a pastor's son—" here she laughed incredulously. "The one that I least expected. And that I'd find a career as a florist, and my flower arrangements would be sold all around the region."

Mary gaped. She imagined she looked like a fish, tossed

out of its natural element and lying breathless on the bank. A Primrose boy! But which one? It wouldn't be Gabriel, as he was too young. That left only Theodore, Simon or Augustus—and Delia marrying any of them was inconceivable.

She supposed she could bear to have Delia marry Simon. She didn't think they were a good match—they were both too distractible. They'd be sure to burn every dinner and put every door on backwards. But she could certainly be happy for her friend sincerely and unjealously.

For Delia to marry Augustus would be horrible for the sheer fact that her friend would have everything Mary had ever dreamed for herself, and Mary herself would be left with nothing. She knew it was wicked to feel jealous but she couldn't help the wrench of her stomach.

Then there was Theodore. Her closest friend. Her confidant. She remembered the way he had gripped her hand when Dr. Hellman had told them the news about Grandma's heart. The kindliness of his brown eyes as they sat on the fence afterwards. The way his calloused fingers must have held the needle as he mended his own clothes. It hurt too much even to consider Delia marrying him. And she couldn't possibly be lucky enough for Camilla's new husband to have a brother.

But then it was almost certain she would marry Theodore, because Theodore was the Primrose that Delia had most detested.

Delia laughed, delighted, taking Mary's expression as excitement and surprise. "You're as surprised as I was! It's better than I could've imagined, since I've long since stopped reviling Theodore and Simon Primrose. And once you stop reviling them, it's only natural to notice how very handsome and gentlemanly they are. Especially Theodore—something about the way he moves," Delia went on, oblivious to Mary's pained confusion as they headed back toward the house. "But don't tell them that part of my destiny. I'd rather tell about the flower arrangements, and leave the rest a surprise, so that things can happen as naturally as possible."

Mary nodded her agreement dumbly, and presently they reached the cottage. Alice had already arrived with her plum wine in hand, and was seated in the kitchen, talking to Grandma through the open door of her bedroom.

"Where are those Primrose boys?" she asked, and both Mary and Delia flushed as though they'd been caught doing something impolite.

It was Grandma who answered from her bed. "Simon's confectionary splendor is more fragile than he thought, and they're looking for a way to move it safely. Theodore stopped by only a moment before you arrived to let me know."

While they waited for the Primroses to arrive, Mary and Delia set the plates out alongside fancy-folded napkins that looked like little white birds in the grass. Then they took Grandma's variously shaped pillows—pink circles, fringed squares, flower-patterned poofs, and set them out behind each plate. Next came the glasses Alice had lent them. They glimmered fragilely among the grass and the pillows and the plates, and would look very charming shining with plum wine.

As they put the finishing touches on the scene—a wreath of pink peonies and roses in the center that Delia insisted on arranging herself—Theodore and Simon came slowly out of the woods, a goat bobbling between them with a towering, three-layer cake with delicate sugar dahlias piped onto the top and sides on its back.

"Dahlias for Delia!" They chorused as they grew closer. With every step the cake rocked precariously, and Simon hovered at its side, his hands stretched out protectively over the sugared flowers. His hair stuck up wildly, and his shirt was streaked with flour. The goat's ears were pinned flat back, and every once in a while it would cast a hopeful peek over its shoulder at the cake, as though gauging the right moment to sneak a bite.

The contrast of the shaggy goat and that splendid cake was a scene in itself, and it set the tone of the party off marvelously. The cake was soon safely secured on the ground, with Delia standing guard against the imagined terrors of swooping birds and wayward grasshoppers, while the rest of the party trooped inside to fetch Grandma.

It was lucky she was very thin and frail these days, because they were able to lift her entire bed right off the ground and maneuver it through the doorframe. They settled her in the shade of the oak tree, at the head of the party, and plumped up pillows behind her head so that she sat up like the Queen presiding from her throne.

All the activity kept Mary's mind happily off the shock of Delia's latest news, but when they settled in to eat, Delia and Theodore ended up sitting shoulder to shoulder, while Mary was sequestered between Grandma and Alice.

She watched them out of the corner of her eye as the first course was served, feeling every easy word between them, every laugh and joke. When she went to take her first bite of turkey—which had been roasted to perfection, with crisp skin on the outside and moist meat on the inside—she found that it had the consistency of sawdust in her mouth. The appetite she had so carefully cultivated the last few months had disappeared altogether.

Everyone else seemed to be having a splendid time. Alice's cheeks grew red from the plum wine, and she told them stories of some of the more memorable times in court—

such as the time one of the lawyers' wigs flew clean off due to his wild gesticulations. Grandma laughed often and loudly from her bed, and tried not to get crumbs in her sheets, and Simon described the making of the cake, which had required several practice rounds that had come to bad ends.

When they sang Happy Birthday, Grandma conducted with two twigs from the oak tree, and Sparrow "roo-roo-ed" merrily along with them, and everyone but Mary was happy as punch.

"So," Delia said to the group at large as she cut the first slice of cake. "Shall I tell you my destiny?" Her dark eyes flashed mischievously to Mary's.

"Yes indeed!" said Alice, sloshing wine into the grass with excitement. "I'm always far nosier than I ought to be about destinies."

There was a pause as Delia made them wait in suspense, and rich cricket song reigned supreme momentarily. At last Delia spoke. "It told me that I will be a successful florist, and sell flowers all around the region! It's the perfect destiny, don't you think?"

On Delia's other side, Simon frowned slightly, and then scratched at his nose. For the first time, Mary noticed that he looked utterly exhausted, with great purple bags under his eyes and his shirt buttoned askew. She wondered if having him make the cake had been too much to ask with all he was doing at the bakery.

But just then Theodore smiled at Delia—one of his slow, crooked, crinkle-eyed smiles. "Sounds like a lovely destiny," he said, and the rest of the group chimed in that it suited her perfectly, and Mary forgot to be worried about Simon because her thoughts were lost to a fresh wave of envy.

Mary felt terrible for the dark feelings brewing in her chest—the jealousy and covetousness that had sprung up so suddenly in her when she ought to be celebrating her friend's birthday. To her credit, she put on such a good face about the whole thing that no one suspected that she was actually sick inside with it all.

When the party had wrapped up and Grandma had been carefully deposited back in her bedroom, Mary ushered everyone off. She wanted to wash up in silence, and then go for a long walk through the pines to try to untangle her thoughts and feelings.

The light was still golden when she set out, the fields glowing with late summer sunshine. She let her feet carry her where they would, paying no mind to where she ended up. It seemed to Mary that the only moral path forward was to put aside her own feelings and support Delia. She wasn't even certain what her feelings were—they were all so confused with the old longings of the past.

But it didn't matter, regardless. Mary had no destiny, and Delia had. So Delia would marry a Primrose boy, while Mary lived with Grandma until the old woman died, at which point she'd be forced to go back to her parents, because it wasn't proper for a girl her age to live out in the woods alone. She'd have to return to life in her second story bedroom, where she wouldn't sweep quite so well in the corners and would sew patterns from books (for surely her imagination would dry up again) and live that way until she became an old maid and died of boredom.

That decided upon, Mary turned around and went back over the hill with a heavy heart. Through the pine trees, the windows of the cabin shone in the setting sun. She couldn't bear to go inside and relive the whole day by talking it all over with Grandma, so instead she went out back to the paddock, and told Rosie the whole situation while she brushed her burnished coat.

Rosie didn't have any advice to offer—often the best confidants don't. She twitched her velveteen ears and gave Mary soulful looks out of her great brown eyes, and chewed her cud thoughtfully. When any light had seeped out of the woods, Mary went back inside, her heart heavy and her mind set on her course of action.

Chapter Thirteen

A FEW DAYS elapsed before Mary's resolution to not get in the way of things for Delia was tested. She was up at the cave behind the waterfall, stowing the jugs of milk that she'd gotten from Rosie that morning.

The cave had rebounded marvelously since its lean winter days—the fat barrels were overflowing with deep orange sweet potatoes and smooth-skinned russets and tiny white fingerling potatoes. Crates held carrots and onions, and garlic braids mingled with meat haunches as they dangled from the ceiling. Grandma had even poured new butter molds before her bedrest, and now the pats were stored on one of the carved shelves in a beautiful array of flowers, next to wheels of cheese wrapped in wax paper.

The bounty of the cave brought Mary deep joy—it was a wonderful thing to see their hard work of the past few months so clearly represented in the food that would sustain them this winter.

She'd just hefted the last of the milk jugs to lift it into its place on the shelf, when she turned to find Theodore waiting politely at the mouth of the cave. The ivy was half draped over one shoulder, and he held a haunch waiting to be hung in one hand.

Mary jumped out of her skin and dropped the jug. Luckily it landed on a mossy bit of rock and didn't shatter—she hadn't heard him come up over the roar of the water.

"Sorry to have frightened you," he shouted, and stepped all the way inside. She smiled at him to show that all was forgiven, and retrieved the milk jug.

He hung his haunch, Mary lingering almost unconsciously as she arranged the jugs on the shelf into a perfect line, and then they both stepped outside.

It was much quieter there, without the roar of the water amplified inside the stone. "Sorry to have startled you," Theodore repeated as they clambered down the rocks. "I said your name, but you mustn't have heard me over the water."

"It's all right," said Mary honestly. She wished that she had heard her name on his tongue—and then immediately felt ashamed at even having the thought. The Mary of old never would have struggled this way. It was those flecks of gold in his brown eyes, making her brain jumbled.

Theo shoved his hands into the pockets of his trousers. "I had actually planned to stop by to bring Grandma Isabella a new book. Do you mind me walking with you?"

"Not at all," said Mary. She wished it weren't so very true how little she minded.

They walked along in silence for a few beats, breathing in the cool pine air that had come in on a northern breeze. And then Theodore broke the silence. "I have to admit, Delia's destiny surprised me." He said it with a careful glance at Mary, to make sure he hadn't hurt her with his talk of destiny.

"Really?" Mary instantly wondered whether he'd

somehow heard the part of her destiny that pertained to him, and was going to tell her that he planned to marry Delia.

"She struck me as the type of person whom fate would want to settle things for. You know—that it would tell her exactly who she ought to marry, along with which career she should settle on. She's such an inconstant person in ways, and I've always noticed that inconstant people have very set destinies, while constant people tend to have wishywashy ones."

Mary laughed, surprised and guiltily relieved that it wasn't an admission of love for her friend. "I suppose that could be the case, though my dad is about as constant as they come, and his was very explicit about what he should do."

"There'll always be exceptions to the rule. Mine is, in a way."

"What is your destiny, then?" Mary asked, curiosity overcoming politeness. Rumors always circulated about people's destinies, but it was considered rude to ask someone directly without the information being offered.

However, Theo didn't seem to mind. He smiled, as though remembering the day it had come, and then fell into the story. "I was so nervous to get it—I was sure that it would tell me to take over the parish for my father, and my entire soul rebelled against doing that. I thought if it did tell me to do so, I'd run away and not stop until I came to a place where people's destinies don't arrive by bird."

"But it didn't. It told me that I should go off into the wildest reaches of the land, and marry a girl in yellow. I was so relieved that I wept during Bible study, and had to be excused. It was easy enough to do the first part right off—I built my cabin with my share of my Grandfather's inheritance, and spent my days exploring every bit of this land I could reach on foot. At first it was difficult to know how to make a living, but hunting and fishing has provided for me, and I love to do it besides. The second part of my destiny has been harder to come by. Many women wear yellow, and yet I've never felt any inclination to marry them."

He paused then, and looked out into the misty woods—the morning mists were always the first sign that fall was coming to Tolling Bell. "But I don't worry about it overly much. I'll know when it's right."

Mary wondered if he was thinking of Delia. She sighed. What a lucky woman his wife would be: evenings by the fireplace with an adventure novel, traipses through the woods on summer mornings, canoe rides over the glimmering lake while Theo fished. "Your destiny sounds lovely. I wish I had any at all—even one that isn't lovely or well suited for me. It would be nice to have something to follow."

Theodore looked down at her, his brows lowered seriously. "Maybe that is why you haven't got one." Mary suddenly felt as though he had come to the reason he'd begun the conversation in the first place.

"What do you mean?"

"Well, you're a very constant person. One of the most constant people I've ever met. Maybe you were better off without a destiny at all, so that you were forced to make your own path."

"Perhaps," said Mary doubtfully. It was a nice way of looking at it, but even Beatrice Mires had gotten a destiny, and she was so constant and saintly a soul that she'd never been late to one appointment in her entire life, while Mary had been late to at least three.

Presently, they arrived back at the cabin. Grandma was fast asleep, so Theo left the book on her bedside table and collected the one she'd finished the day before.

"Did she like it?"

Mary looked up, surprised, from where she'd been putting tea on the stove. "The book, I mean. Did she like it?"

Mary smiled. "She did, very much so. Especially the bit about the pirates." She fiddled with the teapot. When she looked up again, Theodore's steady brown eyes were still on her. Her stomach did a funny little leap. "I was actually going to ask—I've never read a novel, and I thought I might borrow that one now that Grandma is done with it."

Theo stopped short. "Never—" He shook his head, as if to clear it. "Never read a novel!" His excitement grew with every word, and by the end of the sentence he was flinging his hands about. People who love books are always excited for the opportunity to convert non-readers into fellow book lovers, and Mary had stumbled upon one of the devoutest readers in all of Tolling Bell.

A year before, this kind of reaction would have embarrassed her. Now, Mary only grinned, enjoying his excitement.

"Of course you can borrow it! But—no, actually. You can't start with this one. This sort of thing is great for someone looking to pass the time, but it shouldn't be the first novel you ever read. I'll have to think on it." And looking very pensive, the book still tucked under his arm, he walked right out the front door.

When there was a knock on the door an hour later, Mary leapt up again, heart beating fast. She was already imagining what she'd say to Theodore when she opened the door—and found a stooped old woman on the front step.

Her grey hair was wound in a giant knob at the back of her neck, and she was very much not Theodore. It was Mrs. Hellman, the doctor's esteemed mother and one of the biggest church bigwigs.

"Can I help you?" Mary asked politely. She was hesitant

to let the old woman inside. At that time of day the sun poured in through the windows and lit up the dust motes spectacularly—she wasn't sure a person like Mrs. Hellman would see the magic of it.

"I hope you can, Miss Ellmire," began the venerable lady, clasping her wrinkled hands to her great pearl necklace, "I saw Miss Alice Hedelstein's napkins at church last Sunday, and I've come up here to see whether you'd embroider my curtains. I thought maybe you could show me some of your designs, and we'd come up with something together. Something nature-y perhaps, as I can't get out much these days. This walk was quite long enough."

Mary flushed all over with pride and embarrassment and immediately ushered the old woman inside, the dust motes forgotten.

They sat on rockers pulled up next to each other. Mary could tell from the silence in her grandmother's bedroom that she was awake and listening intently. She showed Mrs. Hellman all of her best patterns, even trotting upstairs to fetch a pillow she had recently finished. Finally, a climbing ivy pattern was decided on, and it was arranged that Mary would pick up the linens on her next vegetable round.

"You aren't to lay them in that dirty cart of yours," commanded Mrs. Hellman.

"Of course not," replied Mary, unruffled. "I'll bring a satchel to put them in." And with a proposed price and a handshake of agreement, Mrs. Hellman set off down the path toward town.

Mary would have been happy enough with that, but only the next day there was another knock at the door, and this time Mrs. Dennison stood there, looking rather contrite with her hat pulled low over her brow.

"I saw Judge Hedelstein's napkins at the Church potluck,

and Mrs. Hellman claims you're doing an ivy pattern on her curtains," she began without preamble. "So I wanted to see if perhaps you could squeeze me in as well. I would love napkins like the Judge's, though maybe with herbs instead of bottles."

She had brought her best napkins already, bound up in muslin cloth. Mary agreed, and took them rather dizzily—the curtains would be her biggest project yet, and already she was pressed for time. The vegetable garden was at its peak production and required long hours spent harvesting and canning and making jam from the fruit and drying the herbs and braiding the garlic, so that there'd be stores for winter.

This addition of the napkins would leave her scrambling, but it seemed foolish to turn down an opportunity. When Mrs. Dennison left, Grandma cackled from her bedroom. "Soon they'll all want them, and you won't have time for me and this farmette of ours," she said through the closed door.

Mary rushed in, horrified that her grandmother could ever think such a thing, but Grandma Isabella was grinning. "It's a good thing, child. It lets me know that you'll be alright when I go. Do you know what my biggest regret about having to die is?"

"I don't," said Mary faintly, taken aback by this sudden talk of dying and regrets.

"That I'll have to leave you behind, and miss out on all the fun times that you'll have in your life. We've had splendid times together, haven't we?" She took her granddaughter's hand in her own frail one.

Mary didn't trust herself to speak.

Grandma patted her hand matter-of-factly. "There now. I didn't mean to make you sentimental, I was only trying to tell the truth. Fetch your sewing and get started—I know that you are itching to, and it sounds like you had better get started as soon as you can."

As usual, Grandma's instructions were so sensible that Mary did exactly as she said, and carried her sewing to the foot of Grandma's bed, where she curled up like a loyal puppy and worked out the first stitches of her new herb pattern.

Chapter Fourteen

By the time Theo finally brought a book for her, she had finished and delivered the napkins, started on the curtains, delivered four wagonloads of vegetables, and turned an entire waning raspberry bush into jam.

Every day she'd waited for his knock on the door and been disappointed, and then when he finally did arrive, it wasn't with a knock at all. He marched straight through the open door at breakfast and plunked a book down on the table in front of her, narrowly missing the butter dish.

It was a small, brownish book with a peeling cover. "I won't describe it to you," Theo said as she inspected it. "Books always sound foolish when boiled down to only a few dozen words. You'll just have to read it to find out what it is about, and once you do you'll have to let me know immediately, so that you can tell me what you think."

He sounded so impatient already that Mary laughed. "If you were so excited for me to finish it, why didn't you get it to me sooner?"

Theo sighed. "I couldn't decide which book to give you.

You only get to read a novel for the first time once. Should it be a tale of adventure? Of love? Of good triumphing over evil? Finally I settled on a simple tale—" But he shook his head and cut himself off before he could start to describe it. "Well anyway, I hope it brings you as much joy as it's brought me over the years."

"Thanks, Theo," she said. It gave her a start to say his name aloud. She said it so often in her private thoughts these days that it felt forbidden on her tongue.

He flashed his best crooked smile at her through his wickedly thick beard, and then he was out the door again.

"What was all that fuss about?" asked Grandma from where she was eating her soft-boiled eggs on a tray in the bedroom.

Mary clutched the brown book to her chest for a moment, inhaled the warm leather scent of it, and then went in to tell Grandma all about Theodore and the book.

Grandma flipped through the book absentmindedly. "You've seemed antsy all week— glancing at the door, jumping up at every shift in the wind. I thought you were expecting a gentleman caller, not a book."

Mary flushed, and took the book from Grandma as an excuse to avoid her gaze. The glint in the old woman's eye was far too knowing for comfort.

Sunday dinners of late had been painful for Mary. Only the week after Theo told her about his destiny, Delia happened to wear a gown of sunny yellow, trimmed with gold ribbons, and when the dinner went late and the sun set while they were all still eating, Theo offered to walk her and Alice home.

Mary tried very hard not to feel jealous or sad about the fact that Theo looked mainly at Delia when he offered, but that night a few salty, self-pitying tears slid down the drain along with the dish water as she washed up after them. Her only condolence was that Delia had been asked to start teaching Sunday school after church, and so she usually arrived to their Sunday dinners right before the meal started. This saved Mary from having to hear her thoughts about her future potential husbands—during the rest of the week Mary was too busy with her embroidery and the farm work to escape for a visit with her friend.

Cool drafts had begun to punctuate the heavy, early September air. Usually Mary mourned the loss of summer, because autumn and winter meant bundling up in heavy woolens and sitting in her drafty room to stitch out patterns with shivering fingers.

But on the farm, Mary welcomed the change. She was ready to be finished with her weekly vegetable deliveries and the constant worry and bother of the garden. Autumn meant working on embroidery in front of the wood stove, watching the leaves change from the tops of the hills, heating great steaming mugs of cider for herself and Grandma, and ample time at night to curl up with the book Theo had lent her.

For as she'd soon found, reading by candlelight in the evenings made a welcome change to further work on embroidery. She and Grandma would pull their rockers close to the wood stove and light tea candles on the table and mantel so that they could just make out the cramped black words marching like ants across the respective pages of their books.

I won't try to describe what the book Theo lent her was about—because he was quite right, and summaries never do novels justice. But it was a rollicking tale, full of bravery and goodness. It even had a touch of magic. More than Mary's dust motes and glowing fields perhaps, but less than fairies and elves, so it was easy for Mary to fall headfirst into the story.

She finished it within the week. It was easy when the material was full of lovely characters and villains and mad chases through ancient castles—instead of the dull lessons about morality that she was used to.

That Sunday, Theo sat next to her instead of Delia, so that they could discuss the book. She had loved it every bit as much as he'd hoped she would, and he questioned her minutely about it—what had been her favorite scene? Had she expected who the villain was from the beginning? And what about that part when...?

Afterwards, he was so caught up in excitement with it all that he tore off home to find another one for her. That left Simon to walk Delia and Alice home. He offered in his usual style: with twice the sweetness of Theo, and half the charm.

Theo himself returned soon after the washing up had been finished, Sparrow galloping at his heels with her tongue lolling out of her mouth.

"Now you have to try this one," he said, pressing an emerald tome into her hands. "It's a bit of a slow start, but if you give it half a chance you'll soon feel like you have a new host of friends in the characters."

Mary thanked him, and that night brought it up with her to bed, where she tucked it under her pillow for safe keeping. She was finding that first acquaintances with books were best if not hurried.

That first book had opened a new door for Mary: a world where she could love and laugh and cry with no real stakes for herself. It was better even than having an imagination, because it is so much easier to feel like a story might be real when you can share the imagining with another person.

When the terrible autumn thunderstorms rolled in over

the mountains, Mary and Grandma lit all of the candles, and hunkered in close together on Grandma's bed to read. When their eyes grew tired from reading in the dim light, they told ghost stories and adventure fables of their own invention.

Grandma was a wonderful storyteller. She had a talent for crafting characters that you simply bawled your eyes out over, whether it was a happy story or a sad one.

Some of Mary's happiest times were spent together on that bed, giggling away like two school girls over some foible of one of the heroes (Grandma always liked to imagine that they had flaws hidden beneath their handsomely grim visages—a butt chin masked by a beard, or unfortunate birthmarks).

While the doctor still cautioned Grandma not to overtax her heart, she'd done so well since the last visit that he gave her the okay to putter about the house some, and to sit outside —provided she was well bundled up.

On cool, crisp autumn mornings Grandma would sit outside on her rocker while Mary chopped wood. It wasn't yet time for the wood stove to be put to use full time, but the woodpile required replenishing from last year. It took a day or two, but Mary quickly rediscovered her knack for splitting wood.

Each morning she'd rise with the sun and hurry downstairs to milk Rosie. She sat on the milking stool in the chilly cow shed and rested her cheek against the cow's warm, smooth flank while she milked—trying to absorb as much of her body heat as she could.

Afterwards, she'd come back inside with the milk and eggs, and Grandma would fix them breakfast. Now that the weather had turned cool, she'd begun baking crusty loaves of bread in the stove, and fixing creamy porridges sweetened with jam made in warmer days.

When their bellies had been filled, they'd go outside.

Mary would wield her axe with passion if not precision, while Grandma smoked a big-bellied pipe that puffed out sweet-smelling smoke.

In the old days, Mary would have been scandalized by the mere idea of a woman smoking, but lately she'd tried to redefine her world views not by what was proper, but by what was good. And since she couldn't think of how a woman smoking a pipe would hurt anyone, she decided that it wasn't up to her to have an opinion.

Not that Grandma would've cared if she had had an opinion. When she chided her for doing too much work—trying to stack the wood while Mary chopped or staying on her feet too long doing chores of a morning—Grandma snorted contemptuously.

"The worst thing that could happen is that I'll expire suddenly. And as I know you can provide for yourself now, that doesn't worry me near as much as it did last spring."

Mary shook her head and lined up for another swing. "You make yourself sound like a late library book."

Grandma was right though. In the last few weeks, a half dozen more ladies from the church group had come down to commission sewing from Mary, and she was accumulating quite the pot of money underneath her bed. It seemed she was getting her former wish of becoming a seamstress—though, as is often the case—the work had begun to feel tedious even despite having once been a dream.

"Now come on over to the apple orchard with me, and let's see how those apples are getting along," Grandma said once she'd added this final log to the stack.

Mary obliged, and they strolled over to the straggly line of apple trees that Grandma grandiosely called the orchard. Many of the apples were still small and very hard, but several had ripened enough to eat.

It was Mary's first bite of an apple right off the branch, and the tart sweetness of it simultaneously made her wrinkle her nose and brought saliva rushing into her mouth with the sheer pleasure of the flavor.

One Sunday before dinner, Mary was out in the apple orchard checking to see whether the season for apple pies and tarts and turnovers had yet arrived, when the crunch of leaves behind her made her turn.

She'd been absorbed in dreams of the characters in the emerald book Theo had lent her—this one had taken much longer due to its length and the amount of sewing she had to do these days—and gave a start when she found Augustus Primrose behind her, framed by two rows of apple trees. The brown tweed of his jacket looked very handsome against the craggy trunks of the trees.

"Augustus—" she said aloud. Her cheeks were rapidly becoming as red as the apple clutched in her hand. She'd sometimes imagined Augustus coming to the farm unannounced—and to find him actually here, looking into her eyes with his pale blue ones, left her fully flustered. "Can I help you with something?"

"Delia told me about the Sunday dinner you have with my brothers," he said, adjusting his wire spectacles so that he could peer at her from over them. "I wondered if I might join you."

He always spoke very precisely and carefully, as though his words were made of china and might shatter if he handled them irresponsibly.

"Of course," Mary said at once, even though she knew how little Delia and Grandma liked Augustus. "You're very welcome to join us. Though the rest won't arrive for another half hour at least, and I was only just putting the bread in the oven."

He followed her back to the cabin like a lost puppy, and stood uncomfortably in the kitchen while she popped the bread in and checked on the stew. This stew was from an old family recipe that Grandma Isabella had inherited from her own Grandmother Isabella, and it was one of Mary's favorites —it included chopped prunes, which mixed with the spicy, gingery rabbit meat and savory stock and made for a stew that exploded with flavor.

If Theodore and Simon were surprised to see their brother they hid it well, and gave him big hugs and hearty pats on the back that shook his narrow frame.

"I didn't know you were interested in our Sunday dinners!" said Simon with delight. Simon was the rare sort of person who only grew happier the more relations were present. "We would've invited you long ago if we'd known."

"Well yes," said Augustus, struggling to de-rumple his shirt after the enthusiastic hugs. "When Delia mentioned it at Sunday School I thought that it might make a nice change of scenery from the church. It does sound as though you have fun."

He said 'fun' as though he heartily disapproved of the concept. But then, he had come, hadn't he? Some small, very hopeful voice in the back of Mary's mind whispered that mayhaps he was there for her, and that idea in itself excused all of his other flaws.

Since the ground outside was too chilly to sit on, they'd moved their Sunday dinners back into the cabin. Simon pulled the rocking chairs into the corners, while Mary and Theodore laid quilts and pillows on the ground to protect them from the bite of the stone, and Grandma helped set the bowls out in a big circle on the floor.

Augustus was more useless than Sparrow—who was busy

sniffing hopefully at one of the empty bowls. He followed Mary about stiffly, getting in the way and seeming very skeptical of the whole idea of sitting on the floor.

"It's the only option, isn't it?" snapped Grandma finally. "Seeing as we don't have enough chairs."

Alice and Delia arrived together—Delia with a great big bowl of cabbage salad to complement the stew, and Alice with a bottle of raspberry cordial.

Augustus sniffed at the bottle, even though cordial wasn't even alcoholic. Mary was very grateful when Delia ordered him into action by having him ladle the stew into each bowl—having his stiff presence constantly at her back made her uncomfortable.

Once they all sat down to eat, the atmosphere eased remarkably. Theo and Simon talked with their usual fluidity about all sorts of things—the geese they'd seen migrating in v's across the sky (Theo hoped to shoot one for a Sunday dinner soon), when the first frost would come, and whether Mr. Thomas would get his hay harvest done in time, so that they could buy their year's shipment of hay for the goats and cows.

Augustus was seated between Delia and Alice, and the fact that venerable Alice was so comfortably sitting cross legged on the ground seemed to make Augustus feel better about his doing so as well. He inquired about her friends at the church, and then, as the warm food and comfortable chatter loosened his tongue, bored them all with a parable about a cat that climbed too high into a tree, and wasn't able to get down.

"I've always found that cats are usually quite as adept at getting down as they are getting up," said Grandma contrarily. Theodore caught Mary's eye as he tried to hide a smile in his beard, and she had to bite her lip not to smile as well.

"But that isn't the point," Delia explained to Grandma. "The point is the allegory—that sometimes we climb after goals that are too high for us, and then are unable to lower ourselves to appreciation of the worldly things we've always had."

"Quite right, quite right, that is exactly what I meant," Augustus said pompously.

This time, Theo had to lift his bowl of stew in front of his face to hide the twitch of his lips.

Alice's raspberry cordial caught the candlelight and shimmered splendidly as she raised her glass. "As someone who has both climbed to her highest heights, and remains fully in love with the humble pleasures of the world, I'd like to cheers to the proposition of successfully doing both." That settled the matter completely, because as an esteemed judge, Alice's opinion was always considered absolutely correct by the people of Tolling Bell, even if it was a tad outlandish.

Theodore and Simon gave hearty cheers, and clinked their glasses together so jubilantly that the cordial nearly splashed out.

At the end of the dinner, Augustus offered to walk Delia and Alice home—the church was close to Delia's house, and Alice's was on the way. He thanked Mary very courteously, and asked if he might have the pleasure of making their Sunday dinners a regular habit.

Mary assured him that he'd always be welcome—with a vicious glance at Grandma to keep her mouth closed—and then he bowed over her hand and offered his arm to Delia.

"Goodnight," Mary called after them, and caught a glowing glance from Delia as they melted into the darkness.

Theodore and Simon stayed on to help put the house back to rights—folding quilts, stacking dishes and scrubbing the few wayward droplets of cordial off of the flagstones. "Those Primroses sure are something," said Grandma as she and Mary stood in the doorway to see them off.

"Even Augustus?" asked Mary hopefully.

She snorted. "He's something else."

Chapter Fifteen

It had been some time since Mary had gone on an outdoor adventure, and her legs began itching for a good long walk. In the book Theo had lent her, the characters were always eating acorn-flour pancakes drizzled with maple syrup for breakfast, and so she'd gotten it into her head that she'd like to harvest her own acorns, and try grinding them up from scratch to make flour for pancakes of her own.

The only problem was that it was too early in the season for the oaks in the valley to drop their acorns. Mary's only option was to hike up into the mountains, where winter came to the hillsides sooner, to see if those oaks were dropping. It was a good many miles, and she'd have to dress warmly and bring lunch.

After several days of planning her trip and feeling plagued by uncertainty—Mary had never truly set foot in the highest reaches of the mountains, and blizzards could flare up even in late September—she decided it'd be best to ask an expert's opinion and consult Theodore.

Maybe she could even borrow Sparrow for the trek.

Having the bright little dog along would make her feel infinitely more comfortable.

Grandma was in a state that she couldn't come along. She watched jealously from her rocking chair as Mary packed a satchel full of sandwiches—four towering ones, full of sliced ham and turkey, and toasted bread slathered in butter, draped in Grandma's best lacy cheese and deep green mustard leaves —donned her warmest cloak, and set out for Theo's house.

Theo was out behind his cabin, skinning a deer beneath the wide span of a pine tree. While it was easy to think of him as tame when he was helping Grandma up from her rocker or elbow deep in soapy water, moments like these brought to reality the full force of his wildness, and his willingness to contend with the harshest parts of nature.

His arms were splattered with blood, and he was carefully carving a silvery lining away from a hunk of flesh with a great, curved knife. It looked wickedly sharp.

Sparrow was curled in a sleepy ball at his feet—as Mary approached, the little dog opened her liquid brown eyes and let out a half-hearted, "Roo!" Theo looked round and put down his knife, an easy smile already on his lips. He crossed his arms.

"And what have I done to receive this honor?" he asked once she was within speaking distance.

Mary sank into the leaves at the base of a maple tree nearby—far out of blood spatter range—the skirt of her pink dress tucked carefully over her knees, and explained her mission.

Theo listened with obvious delight—he seemed especially pleased that she'd worked out on her own that she'd have to move to higher altitudes to find dropping acorns this early. "It sounds to me like you've got the itch," he said once she'd finished.

"Excuse me?" asked Mary, drawing herself up prim and proper in a flash.

Theodore's mouth widened with withheld laughter, and he held up an appeasing hand. "I meant the itch for the wild. I have it too—it's what started me down this route. It began with walks in the woods, and grew to long days where I'd wander from daybreak to nightfall. And now they'll call me into their reaches for days at a time, and I'll have no choice but to pack an overnight bag and cozy up with the stars."

Mary nodded, a flush of warmth lingering from the misunderstanding. "I suppose I do," she said thoughtfully. "Anyway, I didn't come to be told I had an itch. I'm looking for your expert opinion on the journey. I've never done anything of the sort alone and Grandma is too frail to come with me. I thought you may even let me borrow Sparrow for the hike, if you can spare her for the day."

"I'll do you one better than Sparrow," said Theo. "You can take the both of us, if you'll have us. I could use a break from cutting up deer, and I'm sure Sparrow would jump at the chance to stretch her legs. I'll give you my expert advice as we go, so next time you're comfortable going alone."

He rubbed his palms on his bloody work pants, and caught sight of his arms. "I'll need to wash up first, of course."

Mary followed him to the front porch of his cabin, and sat on the rocker that looked out over the lake. Sparrow placed her head in Mary's lap, and she absentmindedly stroked the dog's ears.

If she were being honest with herself, she had hoped Theo might offer to come along. She couldn't admit that straight out because it wasn't good of her. Mary had made up her mind not to interfere with Delia and Theo's blooming relationship. And as someone who in the past had always made up her mind and stuck with it regardless of how she felt, it was frustrating to now find herself slipping.

And slip she did. She'd find herself making excuses to go up to the waterfall cave in the mornings to deliver milk, just in case he might be there. Or squeezing extra chapters in at night so that she might finish the book sooner and have an excuse to stop by his cabin with it. Or even walking out in the little open canopied forest near his house, pretending to be looking for mushrooms for dinner.

Theo did seem to stop by often as well—he'd stick his head in of an evening to see how she was getting along in her book. Or he'd come and read aloud to give Grandma a change of pace. Or he'd catch some beautiful, speckled trout in one of the frigid streams up on the mountain side, and he'd want to share it with them for dinner.

But then, Theo had always been around a lot, for he and Grandma were great friends. It was only more so now, Mary told herself, because Grandma could no longer visit him. They had to content themselves with smoking their pipes and swapping tales not looking out over the lake, but gazing along the path that led up the road.

Mary even sometimes wondered if he was coming because he hoped Delia would stop by as well, but that was such a rare event outside of Sunday dinners that it didn't seem likely her friend was the attraction.

Regardless, here Mary was, having thrown herself in the way of spending time with him yet again, only she was ashamed of that fact and what it might mean about her feelings, and so could not admit it to herself.

After a few long minutes, Theo came outside with his face freshly scrubbed and his hands shining and pink. He wore the deep green flannel that disappeared into the woods at dusk and dawn, and his great big clomping-about boots. Sparrow had been adorned with a red handkerchief tied about her neck: "Just in case another hunter might mistake her for a fox," Theo explained.

They set off north, along the side of the lake and toward the ridge of blue mountains against the skyline. Theo slowed his pace a touch, and Mary sped hers up just enough to make up the difference, so that they were soon walking comfortably side by side.

It's very important in an adventuring partner that you have compatible paces. Too big a difference in speed can make an entire venture miserable—for one is always out of breath while the other is constantly bored. Mary was pleased to find that they were well suited for adventuring together— with a slight shortening of Theo's stride, and a slight lengthening of her own, she kept up with ease.

It helped that Theo stopped often to point out natural phenomena that Mary might have missed without him—the little thickets with nests carved into the pine needles where deer slept, skunk tracks in the mud, or a migrating bird that flitted above.

"And keep your eye out for moose," he said during one of those pauses. "They should be going into rut soon, and when they do they get vicious. If one charges at you, don't run, but hide behind a tree."

Mary nodded fervently and memorized that bit of advice.

For her part, Mary had an eye for beauty—she'd stop midstep to gaze wonderingly down a long lane of pine trees, their points austere against the blue of the sky, and Theo would follow her gaze and see beauty in a place he'd long taken for granted as a corridor to prettier places.

Or she'd bend down to peer under a toadstool, and tell Theo how when she was little she had imagined being miniature-sized, and using toadstools as umbrellas during stormy weather. He laughed at these anecdotes, and shared his own—how he'd imagined riding birds like horses, or climbing the crags in the bark of a great oak, and they wondered at the similarities in their childhood imaginings.

The short climb up the foothills left Mary winded—a flush blanketed her cheeks and nose, and against the green of the pine and the red of the needles, notes of red danced in her hair with every step she took.

Theo glanced at her frequently as they climbed, though whether it was admiringly or because he was checking to make sure she was alright was uncertain.

When the ground changed pitch to an even steeper elevation, Mary gasped between steps, "And is this the mountain?" After reading several adventure novels with Grandma, it seemed to her that there was something especially special about the mountain. The mountain was what you had to climb to slay the dragon, or complete the journey, or find safety.

"This is the mountain," said Theodore with a gleam in his eye that hinted he might be thinking along similar lines. "We won't go all the way up it today—the top is bald and only good for views as far as acorns go. But we'll get halfway up, to where the wind chills the landscape."

Mary nodded and bent her head forward into the cold breeze that had already picked up, and together they pushed their way up the mountainside, passing under massive chestnut trees whose shiny nuts threatened to roll their ankles, and delicately peeling birch trees, their white trunks ghostly through the understory.

For most of the hike Mary was too focused on avoiding the snarls of roots and rocks to watch the changing landscape, but every once in a while she'd glance up to find herself in yet another new habitat—and be charmed all over again.

Sparrow, who seemed to have much greater reserves of energy than either of the humans, scarpered through the woods around them—disappearing for long minutes to investigate a scent over the next hill before speeding back to pant at their ankles.

Her missing leg certainly didn't seem slow her down, and by the time they reached a rocky outcropping that gave them views of Tolling Bell ensconced in autumn foliage below, Mary wished she was three-legged herself.

The view was worth any tiredness she felt, though. She had never seen her town from so far away before—in fact, had never been this far away from home except for once, when she'd had a swollen bump on her neck and Dr. Hellman had referred her to a specialist in Brooksville.

But that had been when she was twelve years old, and she hadn't been able to get a view like this from the train.

Mary and Theo sat down to rest their legs and Theo pointed out where the grey stone tower of the church, with the great black bell that had given Tolling Bell its name, jutted through the trees.

They decided to lunch on the outcropping—they'd both fostered a roaring hunger climbing up the first bit of that mountain, and besides, Mary couldn't stop staring at the tapestry of trees and glittering water below.

It was a good thing she'd had the boldness to make enough for two. They were delicious sandwiches to sit in the woods and eat—hearty enough to be satisfying, without weighing them down, and together they ate every last crumb.

They washed them down with long draughts of sweet, cold milk from Rosie, and then continued up the mountain side. Now the trees became shorter and bristlier, except for in the massive ravines that spanned the sides of the mountain. This landscape was equally as enchanting—Mary enjoyed the intricate patterns of the lichens on the rocks, and the frosty looking mosses.

"Moss like this always reminds me of that needlework cushion you did in Grandma's living room," Theodore said, bending down to run a finger over the luscious green carpet of moss.

Mary blushed. "How do you know that I did it?"

"No one makes designs like you do—even my father mentioned the other day that he was thinking about commissioning a new tablecloth for the Church from you." He smiled down at her. "I have no doubt you could make a good living off of it, if you wanted to."

They walked in silence for a moment, Mary feeling the compliment all the way down to her fingertips.

"Actually, you're likely right—I've made enough money to cover all myself and Grandma's expenses this past couple of months. Not that Grandma needs my money..." She trailed off, her gaze on her boots as they navigated a rocky patch that led down into a sunlit glen.

"I sense a 'but' coming."

She smiled. "But—having actually done it for money, I've found that the pressure makes it infinitely less pleasurable. And I *love* to embroider, so I hate to ruin it by doing it for pay."

"What do you want to do, then, if not that? You'll need a way to support yourself... eventually."

Mary's lips turned down. But when she looked into his face and saw only curiosity and kindness in those warm brown eyes, she found herself answering honestly. "If I could choose anything, I think I'd like to be a judge, like Alice."

She watched Theo's expression anxiously, searching for any hint of incredulity. To her relief, she found nothing but excitement in his face. "A judge! That's a marvelous idea,

Mary—you'd be wonderful as a judge. Actually—" he hesitated for a moment, gauging her mood, but then forged on, "I was just telling Simon the other day that you need an outlet for your overdeveloped sense of justice—" He grinned devilishly at her, and offered her a hand down a steep bank formed by the gnarled roots of a maple tree. "It certainly shouldn't come down to arbitrating who gets the largest piece of pie."

She refused his hand, and stepped primly down on her own, though she couldn't stop her lips from twitching as he laughed at her.

It took a bit of searching before they were able to find a white oak dropping acorns, but at last they found one in a ravine. They scrambled down it, and exclaimed in delight over the perfect little acorns that littered the ground everywhere. Theodore was especially excited about the deer sign, and marked the spot down on his map of the mountain for future hunting expeditions.

Mary gathered up handfuls of acorns and shoved them into the satchel. She wasn't sure how many exactly she'd need for her pancakes, but after that beastly hike she wanted to make sure it'd be enough.

When her bag was bulging with them, and Theo's pockets were stuffed full as well, "just to be sure," they headed back down the mountain. This time they walked more slowly than they had come up it. It had been as perfect a day as Mary could've imagined, and she was sad for it to end.

"Well," said Theo when they finally paused outside his front door. She found it very difficult to look him in the eye, afraid he'd read her feelings there. He too was gazing out toward the lake, where red-eyed loons dove beneath the surface of the gleaming water. "I feel I've earned my share of those pancakes."

Mary smiled, suddenly happy again. It would be a few

days before they were ready—she'd have to grind the acorns and soak the meal before she could use them as flour. "You certainly have. I'll stop by on the morning of to let you know when to come."

Theo tore his gaze away from the lake then to look down at her, and the expression in his eyes made her feel suddenly that she didn't fit quite right in her own skin. He reached out and gave her hand an abrupt squeeze with his own very warm, calloused one, and then disappeared inside his cabin.

Sparrow leaned her compact body against her leg as a goodbye, and Mary stroked her soft ears, and then she hurried homeward at last, toward the light shining out in the dusk from her bedroom, her chest clenching with an emotion she didn't dare examine closely.

Chapter Sixteen

MARY FOUND Grandma waiting up for her, her rigid old back propped up in her favorite rocker.

"Delia stopped by while you were gone," she said as soon as Mary had deposited her acorns in a bowl of water and set them in a corner to soak.

"Did she?" Mary asked, surprised and immediately guilty. She looked up to find Grandma watching her shrewdly.

"Yes. She misses you, you know. Feels very lonely without you in town. The girl practically talked my ear off, she was so relieved to have someone to tell things to. This isn't an easy time for her either, you know."

"It isn't?" It seemed to Mary that it was the easiest time in the world.

"Sometimes getting a destiny is as frightening as not getting one, because you suddenly have all these dreadful expectations to live up to, and I bet it's been hard on her to go through it without her best friend."

Guilt dropped into Mary's stomach like a boulder. "I hadn't thought about it that way," she said in a very small voice.

Grandma covered her hand with her own. "She hasn't been the most sensitive friend to you either. But you two love each other, and you shouldn't forget it. Friends are as precious as husbands, even though it may not always feel like it."

Mary's mouth twisted piteously.

"You'll sort it right as rain tomorrow, I'm sure. Now, tell me about your big day! Did you make it to the top of the mountain?"

Mary allowed herself to be guided into the happier topic, despite the knot of shame that pulled only tighter in her breast as she spoke about her stolen time with Theodore.

First thing the next day she set out for town with a basket of soft-boiled eggs, a loaf of freshly made bread, and a little pot of butter. For the final touch, she made up a carafe of hot chocolate, sweetened with honey and thickened with cream.

When she knocked at the Trotters' door, her mother answered only to tell her that Delia was at the church, and should be just finishing up her morning devotional.

It was a pretty walk along Main Street to the church—the great elms that lined the street were decked out in their prettiest shade of yellow, and auburn ribbons fluttered through the air on the tops of the ladies' hats.

Mary realized as she walked that she no longer worried about the pitying glances the townsfolk gave her. Somehow, she had simply stopped caring. She was too busy and felt too beloved by the small circle of friends and family she'd gathered around her to bother with what anyone else thought.

At the church, Mary found Delia pulling her hood up over her head as she stepped out into the chill.

She nearly dropped her bible when she found Mary standing in front of her, basket in the crook of her elbow. Mary smiled apologetically. "Grandma said you'd stopped in, and I was so sad I'd missed you that I set out first thing. Your mother told me you were here."

As soon as Delia recovered from her surprise she beamed, and linked her arm through Mary's. "I'm very glad you did," she said, "I've missed you of late, and last night I felt scared that we were becoming adults so very quickly that our friendship would get left behind like a childhood relic."

"We won't let it," said Mary firmly, and they marched off to find a bench in a sheltered part of the square. When they were seated and out of earshot, she sighed. "I've been a terrible friend to you lately, and I apologize."

Delia laughed. "You've hardly been a terrible friend to me —I've been a terrible friend to you! I told my mother all about how I'd told you about my destiny, and she told me that I'd been insensitive to do so when you hadn't got one, and I've felt so terrible about it for ages but didn't know how to bring it up—"

"You're fully forgiven," said Mary magnanimously. "Meanwhile, I've been so busy moping around about my own misfortune that I completely forgot that it can be hard to get a destiny as well, even a good one."

"You're forgiven as well," said Delia. And then she laughed a hollow sort of laugh. "And let me tell you, you're right. This whole destiny business has been far more trouble than it's worth. How am I supposed to be a florist when it's the wrong season to grow flowers? And how am I supposed to marry a Primrose boy when no Primrose boy will ask me to marry him?"

"Wait, but Delia—there's one more thing I have to confess, and I'm afraid you'll find it very ugly," said Mary, intending to confess all her confused feelings about Delia's husband to be. "I—I've been jealous of you lately. Terribly jealous. With your destiny and a Primrose boy of your very own—"

She braced herself to tell the worst, but before she could begin Delia interrupted her with a laugh.

"You, jealous? And this whole time I've been jealous of you!"

"Of me?" asked Mary, dumbfounded. No one had ever been jealous of her—she'd never had anything that anyone else wanted.

"Yes you," said Delia impatient now for the worst to be known. "You've gotten so very... different lately. Not beautiful, in the way of some girls, but so self-possessed that there is something about you. I even heard Simon Primrose call you "enchanting" the other day to Theodore, and I was always used to being the one who was noticed. I felt ugly about it in my heart, even though I tried not to. And then you seem so very free and happy in your new life—you explore during the days and sew and do all of the things that you love while I am left to try and make something of myself."

Mary was flabbergasted. She felt suddenly very self-conscious, and groped for her glasses in the breast pocket of her dress, but it had been many months and a very different dress since she'd last taken them off. For a moment she wanted to climb back into her window, and away from all the messy humanness of actually living in the world.

But then she let herself hear the word Delia had said Simon had spoken about her—"enchanting"—and she felt suddenly very light and young and happy. She threw her head back and positively roared with laughter.

Across the street, dignified Mrs. Hellman paused in her shopping to cast a scandalized grimace toward them. That Mary Ellmire certainly had grown wild these days.

"So this entire time I've been jealous of you, and you've

been jealous of me, and we've both been holding in all of our troubles and worries until they grew up between us like thorn bushes." She held out her hand, and Delia placed hers in it automatically. "Let's make a pact: we'll never let men or jealousy or destinies come between us again."

They shook on it, and ate their toast and jammy eggs and sipped the hot chocolate, and Delia told Mary all about her unsuccessful attempts to grow flowers, while Mary told her about her latest embroidery projects. By the time they stood up from the bench they were both stiff from cold, and the sun was high in the sky.

"Let's make a regular thing of this," said Delia. "Every Thursday morning."

"Every Thursday morning it is," said Mary. And she went home lighter in her heart than she had been since Delia's birthday party.

Filled with new virtue toward her friend after their conversation, Mary not only let Theodore know that the acorn flour was ready to be made in to pancakes, but she invited Delia for the big breakfast as well.

"Will there be enough for Sparrow?" Theo had asked when she'd stopped by. "I wondered if we'd collected enough acorns."

"I'm not sure there will be," said Mary with an apologetic frown at the dog. "I lost quite a few acorns through my lack of expertise."

"She'll have to be contented with a venison shank at home then," he said, and laid one broad hand on the dog's head.

Mary had gone through quite a process getting the acorns even to the point of edibility. She soon discovered that soaking them for too short a time made them terribly bitter. So she soaked them and soaked them and soaked them, until at last Grandma hinted that perhaps she should try grinding them, and then soaking them. Then the grinding in itself was a labor-intensive process.

Mary had long since begun to feel that these pancakes had better be some of the best ones she'd ever tasted. The characters in her book certainly seemed to enjoy them, but perhaps that was because they hadn't had real flour to compare it with.

The more she ground and fussed and tried to get it down to a usable fineness, the more she worried, until finally she ended up with a fine flour—which was especially luxurious because ounces and ounces of love and hard work had been poured into it. Grandma had been right—grinding and then soaking had been the magic order. When Mary tasted a bit of the meal, at last it had lost its bitter flavor.

To complete the recipe, she brought in the largest, freshest eggs with the orange-est yolks she could find, and Rosie's creamiest milk.

Then she added shaved walnuts and diced cubes of freshly picked apple from the orchard, which was overflowing with apples now. Delia and Theodore arrived just as she was spooling the batter onto the griddle.

Grandma shouted a hallo from her bedroom—she was feeling especially tired today, and had let Mary do the final mix up of the pancakes on her own.

Theo sniffed appreciatively. "Smells like that climb was worth it."

"We'll have to taste them before we know," said Mary, even though her mouth was already watering at the heady smell.

When the first pancake had browned to deep gold color, she pulled it off, and took a sliver off the edge to taste it.

"How is it?" asked Delia, leaning forward in anticipation.

Mary chewed, and then chewed some more. She'd never

tasted a pancake that was so chewy! When at last she could swallow, she frowned. "It's—well, it's....not quite right."

"Is there something wrong with the pancakes?" Grandma shouted from the bedroom.

"Mary says they're not right," shouted Theo through the open door.

Grandma cackled. Moments later, they heard a thump, and she shuffled into the kitchen. She peered at the pancake, which, now that it was off the griddle, was beginning to set into a gelatinous circle.

"I'd add as much wheat flour as you did acorn meal, and double the recipe," she said, poking at the pancake with an expert frown.

Mary gulped. "Really? But then what was even the point of making *acorn* pancakes? Of climbing a mountain and sorting through them all and soaking them and grinding them... My book certainly didn't mention all *that*!"

Beside her, Theo's shoulders started to shake.

"Don't you dare laugh, Theodore Primrose!" she said, poking at him with the spatula.

He couldn't help it—his shoulders shook harder and he wiped tears from his eyes.

Mary couldn't help it either—she started to laugh too. With Grandma's help, soon they had added in wheat flour to the batter, and doubled the other ingredients. This time, the test pancake turned out beautifully—round and gold and fluffy as a cloud.

While she made a tidy stack of pancakes, Theo and Delia sat in the armchairs and caught up on the going ons of the last few weeks.

Mary couldn't help but watch them out of the corner of her eye—even though she had promised she wouldn't let herself feel an ounce of jealousy. They were both very polite with each other, and very careful with how they spoke. It was a contrast to the familiar way Theo handled her—like a sister to be bossed and teased.

When the pancakes were ready, they all sat down at the little oak table to eat. Mary smothered her pancakes in clotted cream, butter, and honey, and the others followed suit. The first bite was exquisite. Perhaps their trip up the mountain had indeed been worth it, Mary thought, relishing the deep nutty flavor of the acorns as it mingled with cream and honey.

"By God," said Theodore, his mouth thick with cream and pancake. He held up a hand to Mary's accusing glance. "I'm not saying the name in vain. These pancakes are a religious experience."

Grandma chuckled. "Wherever I go when I die, dear Lord let there be pancakes too," she said in the facsimile of a prayer.

They each had three pancakes a piece, until their bellies were full to bursting with the richness of it. "I hate feeling over full," said Delia as she dabbed maple syrup off her chin. "But every bite of those was worth it."

Afterwards they all felt too warm and sleepy to venture back outside to their respective homes, so Grandma pulled up her rocking chair to the wood stove and Mary sat down on a pillow while Theo lounged on the floor. Delia took the other rocker, and draped a huge knit blanket over her shoulders to trap the warmth in.

Mary felt so very happy to have them all together that she felt she could bear just about anything at that moment—even if everyone else's happily ever afters unfolded while she was left behind.

Chapter Seventeen

Grandma's tiredness on the day of the pancakes only grew worse as the daylight hours shortened and the calendar days flipped into October. She often felt lightheaded if she stood for too long, and Mary insisted that she no longer try to do even small chores around the house.

Instead, she recruited Theodore and Alice—who was also a big reader—to bring their favorite books and read aloud to her to pass the time.

Mary brought Dr. Hellman again after Grandma felt particularly dizzy one day. He just listened to her heart, shook his head and said, "Let me know at once if anything changes."

So she spent all her time with Grandma now, leaving only for church (where she spent the majority of her time praying that God might spare the old woman a little longer), and her Thursday excursions with Delia, which they'd quickly had to move inside.

Mary was very glad she'd spent so much time chopping wood—they had roaring little fires in their woodstove, and inside, the cottage was cheery and warm. Theo and Simon had graciously offered to take over the farm chores—collecting eggs from the chickens and milking Rosie twice a day—so that Mary could focus all her energy on Grandma.

Outside the cottage, the fields had bloomed into a blaze of yellow goldenrod. Grandma loved to gaze out of the window at the goldenrod, and on milder mornings, Mary would venture outside to gather armfuls of the flowers to fill the house with them. Grandma would squint through the yellow petals and sigh, and Mary knew she was thinking about the days when she could tromp through those flowers on her own two feet.

On a Sunday two weeks after the pancake day, Grandma didn't get out of bed at all. After Mary had cleared up after dinner and sent everyone home, she went bravely through the closed door.

She found Grandma very weak and disoriented. She'd forgotten all about dinner, even though Mary had come in only an hour before everyone arrived to see if she shouldn't cancel it and go to fetch the doctor instead.

"No, no, no," Grandma had said. "I'm just very tired. After a rest I'll be up and about again." It was what she'd been saying all week.

Mary was just settling into her rocker beside Grandma's bed to begin a new novel Theodore had lent them, when there was a knock on the door. It was a self-assured sort of knock— three deep booms.

Mary jumped up at once and went to answer it, and was shocked to find the Mayor standing in the first flurry of the year, his bowler hat pulled low over his eyes as a shield from the wind.

"Is everything alright?" Her mind flew immediately to her lack of a destiny, and all of the terrible things people were saying about her in town. Was he going to make her leave?

"Oh yes, oh yes, everything is right as rain." He squinted up at the sky. "Or snow rather. May I come in?"

She stepped aside to let him in, wishing she had cleared her empty tea mug this morning from her spot beside the fire. Wild thoughts chased each other across her mind—perhaps he'd come to share bad news from town?

When his light grey gaze finally settled on her again, her heart flopped with nerves. "We recently had dinner with the esteemed Judge Hedelstein, and she happened to show us her kitchen linens. Molly was so taken with them that it was all she could talk about for the rest of the evening. Christmas is coming up, and I wondered if perhaps I could commission some from you as a present for her."

He smiled at Mary's expression of relief. "I'd be pleased to," she said once her heart had settled in her chest. "What sort of pattern do you think your wife would like?"

He thought for a moment. "She's quite taken with cats. Especially ones with stripes—we have an orange striped tom and a brown and white tabby. Maybe you could do them in different poses?"

"Certainly," said Mary, though she felt a weariness in her soul at the thought of all those stitches.

"Excellent," said the Mayor. "I'll bring by the linens you're to embroider sometime this week. And it's a surprise, mind you, so don't mention it if you see her."

"I'll be discreet," Mary promised, and then they shook on the deal and she escorted him to the door.

"I can die happy now," said Grandma from the other room with a cackle. "My granddaughter sewing for the mayor himself. And Molly usually shops over at Port Town, where the real retail stores are!"

Mary shook her head, unable to find the humor in death the way Grandma Isabella did.

She slunk back to her spot in the rocker, but couldn't get comfortable, and after a few minutes she slid into Grandma's bed with her.

Her grandmother clasped Mary's hands between her own, her knuckles knobby and sharp through her thin skin. Her hand felt very cold. Mary was thinking deeply, two lines etched between her brows.

"Grandma," she began finally. "I don't think I want sewing to be my career."

"No?" It wasn't often that Grandma was surprised when it came to Mary, but this caught her completely from behind. She had always been such a constant little thing. "What caused the change of heart?"

"I think... it was my dream before I'd ever tried anything else. And now that I've had a taste of the world, I find that I prefer it as a hobby—doing it as a career sounds so *tedious*. And, well, I've been listening to Alice's stories about being a judge, and I think I'd quite like to do something like that. I always have loved rules, and it would be nice to do something good with them, instead of just worrying about what is proper. I've been thinking that I might ask Alice how I should get started."

Grandma chuckled. "That does sound like a very good fit, and I think Alice would be fully delighted."

They looked at each other in the dark room, over the pink-floral sheets on the bed.

"Thank you for telling me," Grandma's voice was very soft.

"It felt like something you should know."

"You've made me very proud to be your grandmother, no matter what it is you decide to do. You're one in a million, Mary."

To someone who hears such things all the time, those

words may not mean much. But to Mary Ellmire, who had spent her entire life being properly part of the pack, they meant the world.

When Mary woke the next morning, her pillow was wet with tears, and she was still holding Grandma's hand. She couldn't remember what she had been dreaming, but she felt oddly calm and content.

She sat up and leaned over to check on her grandmother. The old woman's eyelids fluttered, but otherwise she didn't stir. Mary slid out of bed very carefully, and tiptoed into the kitchen to set the fire blazing again and get breakfast going.

When Grandma still hadn't woken after breakfast, and wouldn't rouse even with a soft touch to the cheek, Mary knew it was time to get the doctor and her parents. She pulled on her warmest burgundy cloak and set out into the gloomy autumn morning.

Dr. Hellman knew by the fierce line of her mouth that it was time. He pulled on his black traveling cloak without a word, and picked up his bulging bag.

"I have to get my parents," said Mary faintly.

He nodded and set out at once down the street, the overcast sky lower and lower over his head until it swallowed him up into fog.

Mary's boots slid on the damp cobblestone as she hurried through the square and onto the narrow street against the foothills that harbored her childhood home. Her mother and father were only just rousing for the day. She found her father kneeling before the wood stove in his threadbare slippers.

"Father," she began tentatively, "Grandma isn't doing well. Dr. Hellman is on his way over now, but I think you ought to come as well."

He looked up, face grey and grave in the early morning light. "I'll fetch your mother." Mary nodded and wavered in the doorway. Politeness dictated that she wait for her parents to dress and don their cloaks and fuss with the fire so that she could walk with them. But Grandma was waiting at home with only the doctor there if she woke.

"I've got to fetch another couple of people. I'll meet you there." Her father only bowed his head as he swept out of the room, and Mary was free to trot down the street unencumbered.

It wasn't at all polite to invite anyone more than the immediate family to the deathbed of a family member, but she didn't care. The Sunday dinner crew loved Grandma as much as any of her family, and they deserved their goodbyes.

Alice went quite pale at the news and hurried off down the street at once, but Delia took a deep breath and pulled on her cloak with a resigned air, ready to face whatever tragedy came at her friend's side.

They walked back together, Delia gripping Mary's hand in a comforting vice. The cabin was a cheery little speck of brightness through the dark trees—candles glowed in the windows, and a dark huddle of people waited at the front door. When they'd arrived, Mary hurried inside and sent Delia off into the woods again to fetch Theodore and Simon.

Soon the whole party was present, only it was very different than their usual meetings. Everyone spoke in quiet, hushed tones and no one had brought any food.

Dr. Hellman informed her that Grandma's time was imminent, and that all they could do now was wait. With those words, the calm that Mary had experienced was whipped away by the terror of it all, and she floated adrift on a wind of sorrow and loneliness.

She retreated to a rocker in the corner, and hardly noticed when Theo draped a blanket over her shoulders. Simon, realizing that everyone had missed breakfast, cooked up a dozen eggs, fried up some day-old bread from the bakery, and laid out bacon in thick slabs over the stovetop so that they sizzled merrily and lightened the atmosphere.

And while none of them felt hungry at first, the bacon smelled so good and Simon was so gentle in offering it that no one could resist taking a slice or two, and piling into Grandma's bedroom to tell her about all of their favorite memories with her, even though she was sleeping still and couldn't seem to waken.

Sparrow even curled up in bed with Grandma and licked her cheek when everyone else fell silent.

At first Mary's parents hung back—they weren't a usual part of the Sunday dinner crew, and were stricken by the impropriety of it all—especially the fact that two of the Primrose boys had been invited, and that they had brought the three-legged dog with them.

But when they saw how lovingly each person spoke to Grandma, and how white faced or teary-eyed each was, they understood that Grandma's family circle extended wider than blood relations.

So they got themselves some eggs and bacon and sat down to join the talk, and her father made everyone chuckle with his stories of the days when he was a child and Grandma had been as prim and proper as they came.

Mary's mother cooked a supper of pot pie—thick with mashed potatoes, mushrooms and peas—and before they could eat it, Grandma died.

She did it in her sleep, just as they all headed into the kitchen again to collect their plates. Dr. Hellman called them hurriedly back.

They each kissed her wrinkly old cheek in parting, and then Dr. Hellman covered her in one of her floral sheets, the one that only last night she and Grandma had whispered across. Mary gulped with sorrow as it covered that beloved face.

She was very distant as her mother and father spoke to each other in hushed tones, and the party dispersed with tears on their cheeks. Her parents tried to get her to come home with them that night—they didn't think it was a good idea for a young woman to stay alone in a cottage in the woods after such a traumatic day, and they likely were right, but Mary refused to budge from the little house.

"This is my home now," she said. "And besides, Theodore will stay around for an hour or two to look after me."

This didn't particularly comfort them, but Mary seemed to have absorbed some of Grandma's obstinacy, and couldn't be budged on the matter.

They left when all the arrangements had been made, and Grandma had been shifted into a wagon to be brought to the undertakers, still under her pretty floral sheet. She would be brought back to be buried out in her scraggly orchard—where she had specified in her will.

It wasn't until Mary and Theodore were alone that she was struck by the terrible finality of it. Everything in the house was another reminder of how very permanent death is. Grandma would never milk Rosie again. Or sleep in that narrow, rickety bed. Or fill up the knobby blue vase with flowers she'd cut from the garden.

Never again would she and Mary curl up under her quilt to tell stories. Never again would she give Mary advice or laugh at her outdated ideas. What would she do without her? How could she ever go on?

Grief, she realized, was pain so sharp and large that it became almost sweet. In missing someone so dearly, you cannot help but recall all of the best parts of them and force yourself into missing them even more deeply.

It was then that the tears came, great, shoulder shaking sobs that left her wretchedly red-eyed. Theodore sat down beside her on Grandma's bed and took her hand in his great big warm one.

He didn't say anything, just held it. And he had the courtesy not to look at her while she cried, which is a true marker of just how good and kind he was, because most people can't resist a peek at a person caught in the spoils of grief.

Mary was too absorbed in her own grief to realize that tears slipped silently down his nose as well, before disappearing into his beard. If she had been able to step away from herself for a moment, she would have realized that Theodore had known and loved Grandma at least as well as she had.

The sun set before Mary's tears dried up. Theodore extracted his hand from hers and rose, his knees creaky after the long hours of sitting. Then he put a pot of tea on the stove, and chopped up an apple and some nuts.

"You'd best have something to eat," he said, voice hoarse. He delivered her the mug and plate. He seemed to expect her to protest—perhaps he had heard stories about how she'd behaved after her eighteenth birthday.

But she took the food and drink meekly, and nibbled at the apples without much appetite, but with determination. The tea especially warmed her. It was the same familiar brand that Grandma had always drank.

They sat in silence as Theodore ate his own apple: unsliced, in giant bites from bottom to top, core and all. Then he cleared his throat. "So," he began, sounding distinctly awkward. "What will you do now?"

Mary understood that it was a question that he had to ask if he was to be a good friend to her, even if it was painful for her to think about. "Before, I thought I would go back to my parents," she said after a moment of consideration. "But the idea of living in that bedroom in that house is intolerable to me now. I think I will stay on here. Someone needs to take care of Rosie and the garden."

Theo nodded, unsurprised. "I'm sure you'll manage quite nicely. But please don't hesitate to call on me if you need anything at all."

Sparrow nudged her nose into Mary's palm as though echoing the sentiment. "Thank you, Theo—and Sparrow," she said, smiling down at the dog. When she looked up Theo's eyes were on hers, and such a very soft brown that they reminded her of velvet. For the first time that evening, she realized how very alone they were. A searing heat slunk up her neck and into her cheeks.

Theodore cleared his throat. "Well, goodnight," he said, and in a blink he had disappeared out the door, Sparrow's white-tipped tail flashing out into the darkness behind him.

Chapter Eighteen

THE NEXT WEEK was difficult for Mary Ellmire. She kept thinking of things she'd like to tell Grandma, and then realizing all at once that she'd never tell her anything ever again. The nights were frightfully long with only grief and longing to keep her company, and the cottage was terribly quiet during the day.

Mary cried into her porridge each morning, and her voice often cracked as she coaxed Rosie into letting down her milk. The poor cow was taking Grandma's loss especially hard. The day after Grandma died, she even kicked over the milk bucket.

"This is hard for me too!" Mary had cried as she desperately tried to salvage what was left in the bucket, and Rosie had twitched an unsympathetic ear back toward her.

At one point during a long, sleepless night, she caught a glimpse of the sickle moon through her window. It winked through the trees at her, gleaming and slender against the velvety expanse of sky.

Mary remembered lying in bed the day after her destiny had failed to come. At the time, she'd thought it was the darkest moment of her life. She laughed—a choked, pitiful sound almost lost to the chirp of the crickets outside. She'd known so little back then.

A surge of gratitude washed over her for all that Grandma had shown her. When she thought about that summer, it was a blaze of sunshine and color and laughter—a bright spot in an otherwise colorless life.

Grandma had woken her to all of the wonderful things about being alive: good food and friendship and adventures. Freshly picked flowers, and laughter, and hot coffee on a cold morning. And love—real, raw love for another person, flaws and all.

She loved her parents, of course, but they had always been removed from her—idols for how adults should act and behave, instead of humans with their own particular peccadilloes.

However, with love comes loss. And now, again, Grandma was teaching her just how dark and messy the human existence could be.

Her heart squeezed with pain at the thought, and she curled up so that her tears would have a shorter distance to fall before soaking into the fibers of her pillow.

She succumbed to the darkness for three whole days—allowing herself to move through her daily chores in a haze of pain and regret. And then she thought about what Grandma would want for her—what she would say if she could see her only granddaughter moping about the house.

The next morning, instead of curling up by the stove to stitch, Mary washed the dried tears from her face. She dressed in her soberest woolen gown, and pulled on her warmest cloak. The walk into town was long and cold, but Mary was determined. Outside the thick oak door, she squared her small, stern shoulders, and knocked.

"Come in," called a voice, half-distracted and familiar.

Alice was seated behind an imposing wooden desk. Stacks of paperwork sat in a neat pile next to a fountain ink pen, and a great wooden grandfather clock ticked the seconds away in the corner.

"Have a seat, deary," said Alice, her face transforming from abstracted thought into sympathy at the forlorn little figure across from her. Mary slid awkwardly into the stiff wooden chair on the opposite side of the desk. She couldn't help but tap her foot, a sound that echoed nervously against the wood paneled walls of the room. "How are you holding up?"

"I—" began Mary, but her voice cracked, and to her horror, her eyes began to fill. She stopped, swallowed. "I'm fine." She sounded anything but fine, and the pity in Alice's eyes. made her hurry forward. "But I'm here because—because I think I'd like to become a judge."

It wasn't at all what she had planned to say, which was more like an essay as to why Alice should consider her, and less like a wishy-washy statement. Trying to recover, she hurried on. "After you said I'd be good at it, the thought kept popping up in my mind. I'd like to do something other than be a seamstress. I want to help do real good in the world."

The judge's face was still for a long moment, considering. It wasn't the delight and excitement Mary had expected, but somehow better, because it meant Alice took her seriously.

"I did mean it when I said it," she said finally. "But it will take work on your part." The words were stern. "Study of the law, both formally and informally, and apprenticeship with a judge—"

Mary's heart leapt unpleasantly. She had thought it was clear that she was asking Alice to take her on. Certainly no one else would, not without a destiny. But she soon breathed free, because Alice continued on to say, "I'll take you on, of course, unless you'd like to study with Judge Magee from Wilmington. He's very good."

"Oh no," said Mary. "I'd much rather study with you. And I don't mind hard work. If I've learned anything in the last year, it's that."

Alice looked at the grim young woman sitting across from her, the obstinate angle of her chin so reminiscent of her grandmother. A smile broke through the firm lines of her own face. "It's settled then. We'll begin next week."

They shook hands, and Mary got up to go with the first bud of happiness blooming in her chest since Grandma had died. Grandma had been right—she could take care of herself, even if it was difficult and scary sometimes. She wished more than ever that she could tell her all about it.

"I'll see you Sunday," she called, donning her cloak. "And thank you!"

She caught a flash of Alice's smile before she stepped out into the chill fall air.

SUNDAY WAS to be Grandma's funeral. Mary's parents had made the arrangements, but Mary had insisted on certain tweaks—that it take place at the little cottage, that they do it in the style of a Sunday dinner, with each person bringing something to share, that they all wear bright cheery colors instead of black, and that she be allowed to handle the flower arrangement, with Delia's help.

In any other instance they would have refused to comply with her demands, but she had such a dangerous gleam in her eye that they worried she might dive off the deep end if they argued—and they were still hoping she would come home after the services were completed. And so Grandma's funeral was shaping up to be as unconventional as her life had been.

On the day of, Mary roasted a venison flank in a fruity red wine and chunks of garlic that had been dried the year before. She had traded a knit blanket with Theo for the flank—a thick green one that would look well draped over his sofa. He hadn't wanted to take it, but Mary had obstinately insisted.

When the flank was safely secured in the belly of the stove, Mary trooped outside to the fields, where she gathered armful after armful of golden rod until her eyelashes and hair were thick with pollen.

The sun was shining this morning, and Mary squinted up at the sky through her yellow lashes and turned the sky into a blaze of gold, and felt if not happy, at the very least free.

Theodore, passing through the darkest part of the woods with an apple pie held snugly in his mittened hands—on his way to deliver it to the cottage—caught the glimmer of yellow in the corner of his eye and stopped in his tracks.

Mary had twisted her hair up into thick braids on the back of her head, and she wore Grandma's royal purple cloak. In the powdering of yellow she glimmered like one of the elusive wildflowers he loved so. Her expression was wild and raw, like the bitterest and sweetest parts of a winter wind. For all his stillness, Theo's heart beat very quickly in his chest.

After a long moment, he tore himself away and retreated back into the shadows, toward the haven of his little cabin on the lake, the apple pie still clutched thoughtlessly in his hands.

Meanwhile, Mary came out of her revery and blinked the pollen off of her eyelashes and onto her cheeks, completely unaware that a great change had been wrought in her life. She shook her head, and towed her bounty of flowers into the house.

By the time the first guests arrived, yellow flowers burst out of vases and were twined around the railing that led up to Mary's bedroom.

Mary had even twined a wreath of them—they looked very well perched on top of her head, and brought out a reddish tint in her hair.

The first guest to arrive—the punctual to a fault old Mrs. Hellman—thought that Mary Ellmire looked rather more like she was attending a wedding than a funeral, but that she certainly had come into herself in the last year. She herself was clad in a sober black gown, despite the instructions.

Shortly after, the Trotters arrived. Even Mr. Trotter had gotten into the spirit, with a deep burgundy shirt and emerald suspenders, and Delia and her mother looked elegant in similar shades of pink.

Augustus Primrose and Pastor Primrose arrived together. They both wore black shirts, but Augustus at least had added a cheery yellow bowtie to his collar. Pastor Primrose looked around the little cottage with deep wrinkles of concern carved between his eyes—there was not a cross or bible to be seen.

But then, he hadn't been asked to preside over the funeral —he was there strictly to support his sons—and Isabella Ellmire hadn't attended church in many years, so it was only to be expected. Besides, she had been a good woman, even if a bit unconventional.

After that it was a steady trickle: Mary's parents, Alice, Dr. Hellman, Simon and the youngest Primrose, Gabriel, and his girlfriend, Annie. Even the Mayor put in an appearance, though mainly because he felt he ought to after hearing that he had stopped into the home while the elderly Ellmire was dying and hadn't even noticed.

Just prior to the funeral, a whole crew of the poorer townsfolk appeared, herding their children ahead of them, dressed in their brightest frocks and wearing tears on their cheeks already.

"Your grandmother was the kindest woman I've met in my life," said Mrs. Bedwin, a thin, sickly woman whose flock of children had already dispersed into the crowd. Only the youngest still clung to her skirt.

"She truly lived out her values," agreed Mr. Bright. "When I was at school, she always made sure I got lunch when Pa was off his rocker, and it only took one stern glance from her to stop a bully in his tracks."

Mary thanked them heartily for the stories, and silently resolved more than ever to keep up Grandma's tradition of bringing vegetables around.

When the appointed time had come, two o'clock, they all trooped out to the orchard. Theodore, who had appeared at the last moment, offered to be one of the people to help lower the coffin down into the ground. Tears streamed freely down his cheeks and soaked into his beard—which he had trimmed for the occasion so that he looked almost genteel—and made the throats of everyone else tighten as they thought of what a grand old dame Grandma Isabella had been to tame such a wild man, and how many wonderful adventures she had had.

Mary herself stood in the front of the mob, her arms hugged tight about herself as though to keep her body from breaking into pieces, and in her sorrow she looked so very beautiful and fierce that several of the young men in the bunch couldn't seem to keep their eyes off of her.

Theodore on the other hand, didn't look at her once, and kept his head carefully bowed when she stepped up to say a few words to the crowd.

When everyone had said their piece and the Primrose

boys had buried Grandma Isabella peacefully in the ground in her beloved orchard, everyone squeezed into the cabin, now very cold and very hungry.

Soon thirty people were feasting on a hodgepodge of mismatched dishes and drinking great gobletfuls of cider and wine and beer until warmth returned to their cheeks and they felt merry and wanted to share all their fondest stories of Grandma.

And the stories were wonderful—tales of Grandma bringing blankets and food on cold, hungry Christmases—shooting a goose on the Mayor's land only to scoff at him when he chided her, and inviting him to share in the feast of roast goose—and perhaps her crowning achievement: the time she had dove into the river in her skivvies to rescue the littlest Bedwin from drowning.

Mary was fascinated to hear about her earlier days—Mrs. Hellman told them all a story about their days as school girls together, and how Grandma insisted on saying the prayers just so when they took their midday meal.

Mary's dad laughed heartily at that. "She used to be a real stickler for the rules—I'll never forget the spanking she gave me when she caught me sliding down the banister..." Her father trailed off, and Mary looked up to find both her parents watching her. Her mother's forehead had gathered into a worried crease.

Mary mustered a smile, and laid a hand on her mother's arm. "I'll be okay—even if I am a bit like Grandma."

Her mother squeezed her hand, and guided her gently toward the table, which was laden with food, and away from the crowd of listening ears. "You'll come home with us tonight, won't you Mary?" she asked tentatively.

Mary's chin lifted unconsciously. "I can't. I need to stay here, to milk Rosie and care for the chickens. They need me out here, mother. You and father get along just fine without me."

Before her mother could say another word, she turned to the table, to begin clearing away dishes. She had just set eyes on Theodore's apple pie—still wrapped in its blue checked cloth—and went to unwrap and slice it, when she realized its maker was missing.

She stumbled for a second—she was so used to him being there when she needed him—but then went on handing out his pie. She would've had a slice herself, but her appetite had disappeared, and she regretted eating a second ham sandwich from the platter the Trotters had brought.

The party ate and drank well into the night, but Theodore still didn't show. It seemed very odd for him not to be there— he had known Grandma best of all in the last few years of her life, and had some of the best stories about her. But then, perhaps he had needed quiet time himself, to digest Grandma's death and say goodbye to her.

Mary felt suddenly very selfish for not checking in on him as he had for her—she had been so wrapped up in what Grandma meant to her that she'd forgotten that she had also belonged to the whole rest of the town.

That evening, Delia hung back to help her clean up after the mayhem. "You're very brave to live out in this cottage alone," she said as she straightened the cushions on the rockers, "I'm not sure I could do it, even with another person around to keep me company."

"It's lonely at times, I won't deny it," said Mary as she scrubbed a pot. "But I've come to love my freedom too much to give it up. There's something so refreshing about being able to do what you like when you like it, without the public eye upon you."

Delia sighed. "That does sound nice, I suppose. Very

different from—" she hesitated and cast a sly eye toward Mary. "What would you think about living in a rectory? I sometimes think it could be very pleasant, even if you are in the public eye."

Mary looked up sharply at that, wondering if Delia had guessed her secret past desires and whether perhaps Augustus had said something to her at Bible study. "I'm sure it would be," she said, but there was a fragile edge to her tone that ended the topic altogether.

When everything had been cleared, Delia set off into the darkness alone even though Mary offered to walk her home, her deep black curls hidden under the petal pink hood of her cloak. Mary felt very unsettled. The cottage was empty, and she wished so strongly that she could tell Grandma about the funeral that she finally went out to Rosie, and leaned her cheek against the cow's neck to tell it all out.

Before she knew it, her mouth was dry with all the words that had spilled free from her, just as she'd have told them to Grandma—all about the flowers and the stories and the people who had turned out in droves to wish her well and her mixed feelings about Delia's question, and how Theodore had disappeared. Afterwards she felt infinitely lighter, as though an invisible load had been lifted from her shoulders. She gave Rosie a hug and went inside to sleep.

Chapter Nineteen

TELLING all of her thoughts to Rosie became a nightly tradition for Mary. It was a good thing she had the cow, because Theodore seemed to have disappeared just as suddenly as he had come into her life.

This dampened her evenings as well, because she wasn't able to swap the novel she had recently finished for a new one. She had stopped by several times to check in on him, but he never seemed to be home. The door was closed firmly to the wind, and no smoke curled from the chimney. Worse yet, that friendly little light that had shone in his window had gone out. Mary felt a bit as if she had lost two friends, instead of just one.

She was very glad for the distraction of her new studies with Alice, because the days at the cottage were very long and lonely, even with Rosie to tell things to.

Three times a week she did the milking and collected the eggs and then changed into her soberest grey gown. The walk into town was long, cold and often dark—the sun didn't come up until well after Mary rose in the mornings now that it was November—but she didn't mind it.

Being alone in the shadows suited her mood these days.

Alice always lit an oil lamp for her, and set it in the window so that Mary had something to guide her on the earliest mornings, and she'd creep into the great, ancient smelling house and slip into Alice's office.

Each visit, her new mentor would pull down a dusty law volume and set Mary to reading a chapter while she poured over paperwork from court the day prior, and then they would discuss what Mary had read, and Alice would stress the points that she ought to most remember while Mary scribbled furiously.

Alice was a patient teacher, but a strict one, and she was not one to let weak understanding of a concept pass by uncommented upon. When Mary seemed not to understand something she'd halt the entire lesson to backtrack to the beginning points. And usually, after some humiliation, Mary would grasp the point.

In Mary, Alice found a hardworking, eager pupil. She certainly wasn't perfect—she often required explanation of any concept that related to a world larger than the little village of Tolling Bell—having never visited any other area—and she sometimes struggled with the less tangible ideas.

When she learned that you couldn't marry just anyone in towns where destinies didn't arrive by bird, she was completely flummoxed. She couldn't believe that it was illegal for men to marry men, or women to marry women, or for people of different races to marry. And when she learned about segregation, she spat out her tea, all over Alice's papers. Her schoolteacher certainly had never touched on the horrific laws that Black citizens were subject to in other places. Her and Alice spent the rest of that day blotting tea up from the desk, and recopying the papers, Alice patting her consolingly on the back every time she apologized.

Like any beginner, Mary immediately wanted to get started—she couldn't wait to begin judging real cases and bringing real good to the world, not to mention going to court to watch the lawyers argue and the jury waver and Alice bang her gavel—but Alice insisted that she would bring her soon enough, and in the meantime she must first learn the elements of law.

So she read and discussed and wrote, and learned a great deal while developing a stiff neck from so much bending over books.

When Mary wasn't studying with Alice, she spent the days embroidering for the Mayor's wife. It was fine, nit-picky work because she wouldn't settle for anything less than the best, and often had to pick stitches out to redo them to her liking.

One cold, brilliant afternoon, she was cozied up next to the wood stove, working on a tricky corner where the cats' tails twined artistically, when a knock at the door made her stick herself with the needle.

She opened the door and blinked in the bright light. Augustus Primrose stood just outside, hands clenched behind his back. His face was pastier than usual—his lips almost purplish in the cold.

"Hello, Mary," he said.

"Hello. Would you like to come in?" Mary asked. She was very perplexed—she had been expecting the eldest Primrose when she'd heard the knock on the door and had been disappointed when it was Augustus instead of Theodore.

"I wondered if you might like to go for a walk." His voice was tight, and it dawned on Mary that he was nervous.

Her nerves sparked as if lit by his. What could he have to tell her on a walk? Walks were traditionally romantic propositions—meant for couples to escape from the listening ears of their relatives to hash things out. Not that Mary had any relatives here to eavesdrop. Suddenly, she wished Grandma were here to forbid her from going out alone.

Not having any crotchety relatives to protest on her behalf—and too polite to protest on her own behalf—Mary had little choice.

"Certainly," she said, patting her suddenly sweaty palms dry on the skirt of her dress. "Let me just grab my cloak." The wind whipped at her hair and clothes as she stepped outside.

The weather certainly wasn't ideal for a serious conversation of any kind—they'd have to shout to be heard over it.

Mary led Augustus toward the woods behind the cottage, where the wind would be softened by foliage. For long minutes they walked in silence, leaves crunching beneath their boots. And then Augustus began.

"Mary." The sound of her name sent a jolt through her body like a shock of static. "I have something to ask of you. Something serious."

"Yes?" she asked rather breathlessly. For a moment her old fantasy about marrying him eclipsed all that she had learned about herself. She felt flattered and confused—and it wasn't as though Theodore wanted to marry her, anyway, so why shouldn't she marry someone else? Even if he may not be the right person?

"Recently I have begun to have feelings—for Delia. I have asked her to marry me, but she says she won't marry me because she promised you she'd never let a man come between the two of you, and she thought you might have feelings for me."

The daydreams crashed down around her ears with the name of her best friend. "Oh," she said very faintly.

"I was hoping that if you gave your blessing, she might change her mind."

"Does she care for you as well?" Mary heard herself ask. But it was a silly question. As soon as she asked it, she knew. She remembered the way Delia had mentioned that it might be nice to live in the rectory. Now that she looked back on it, she saw that Delia had hoped she might say she didn't want that sort of life, so that she'd be free to marry Augustus.

And the way Delia had brought him to all of the Sunday dinners, even though he fit so poorly into the bunch. And how she had suddenly taken up spending so much time at the church, when she had never been known to do so before.

The pastor's son you least expect, her scroll had read. Yes, even that made sense. By the time her destiny came Delia had already been quite fond of Theodore, and Mary distinctly remembered her saying that it would be a dreadfully bad destiny to have to marry stuffy old Augustus.

She laughed—a dry, wry laugh that her old self would have been completely horrified at. But it was better than sobbing, and at that moment she wasn't sure which she would do. And there was still Augustus to attend to. Augustus, who had given a little start at the sound of her laugh and now hung his head, dispirited.

"If it will make you both happy, I can't hesitate in giving you my blessing. But perhaps Delia will need to hear it from me. Send her along, and I'll talk her round."

Augustus' slender shoulders hunched with relief. "Oh that'd be excellent. Thank you, Mary! I've always thought you were a splendid woman, I really have, even if my father does think you've brought your destinylessness on yourself."

That comment would have ruined her a year ago, and while it wasn't pleasant to hear now—it is never pleasant to hear that someone you once respected disdains you—she was able to smile it away by imagining what Grandma might say.

"It's no trouble," she said, and hurried him back toward

the path. She wanted desperately to be alone so that she could examine her thoughts on the matter without having anyone else there to dissect her expression.

"Good day!" he called as he hurried away again, and for the first time Mary thought that he actually meant it.

She closed the door between herself and him and sank down into the rocker again, her chin resting on her chest—just as Grandma had used to sit. Yes, there was that kernel of sadness she had been waiting for. It was small and hard, and lodged just beneath her breastbone, in the tender area reserved for things like children and husbands.

But it was smaller than she had expected. It was a very different Mary who had dreamed of marrying Augustus Primrose.

And it couldn't rival the warmth that had bloomed inside of her from the thought of Delia's loyalty and kindness. It was a golden friend who turned down a man she loved just because she had made a promise. Mary wasn't sure that she could have done it herself.

That evening just before sunset, another, quieter knock sounded on the door. Mary got up this time knowing who to expect. Delia was outside, radiant in her softest muslin gown, a heavy woolen cape draped over her shoulders to ward off the chill.

"Come in," said Mary at once, and she was able to smile with real warmth. She put on a pot of tea, and then they warmed their hands on the mugs and nibbled sugar biscuits while Mary insisted that Delia ought to marry Augustus. "I want more than anything for you to be happy," she said finally. "And I'd be miserable if I thought my own insubstantial feelings had prevented an entire life of bliss for you."

Delia flew up from the table and wrapped her in a hug. After that they moved on to the specifics—Delia told her how she had never liked Augustus. She had agreed with Grandma at first when she called him a primpy little shrimp. But then she'd begun going to morning devotionals out of loneliness, when Mary had moved out to the country, and she'd had to spend more time with him. When he'd asked her to help teach Sunday school, she'd said yes—half because she liked his company.

Often they planned lessons beforehand side by side, and Augustus would give her tips on how to keep the children entertained throughout. "He is so sweet with them—much more comfortable and charming than he is with adults," Delia smiled wistfully. "He always knows just what to say, and how to say it. I couldn't help but begin to soften toward him, though I fought with myself to prevent it, because I knew that you had used to harbor affections for him."

Mary bowed her head.

"But it was very hard to keep away from him, and I found myself wanting to spend more and more time at church. There's something about teaching God's word that helps one to better understand it—" she drifted off dreamily for a moment.

"Yes," interrupted Mary dryly. "Or perhaps it just helps to have a handsome pastor's son reading it to you."

Delia laughed. "I suppose that could've been it. Oh but Mary—he really is so much better than I ever thought he was. So kind and considerate and hardworking. I used to think that the Primroses did something wrong in the upbringing of their children, but now that I know them all, I've fully changed my mind. They did a splendid job, even if Pastor Primrose is a bit of a stick-in-the-mud."

Mary flushed at the thought of what Pastor Primrose thought of her.

"Anyway, finally Augustus pulled me aside after Bible

study and asked to take a walk up the church tower with him to see the bells. I didn't suspect a thing at the time, truly. Up and up we went, and then when we got to the top I hadn't even had time to catch my breath before he'd dropped to one knee and asked me to marry him. He had a ring and everything, a beautiful square sapphire. I was sorely tested, I'll admit it. But I told him that I couldn't, because I had promised never to let another man come between us, and I remembered your old dreams about what your destiny might be like."

Mary nodded. "You're a stronger woman than I," she admitted, thinking of all the times she had purposely run into Theodore even when she had suspected Delia might love him.

Her heart lifted. Theodore! All of this meant that Delia didn't love him—that Delia wasn't the woman in yellow he was meant to marry. And he may not love Mary, but at least she was now free to love him in peace.

She couldn't stop the smile from running over her face like cracked yolk over toast. "I'm happy for you," she continued truthfully. "So very, very happy for you."

"Oh I'm glad you are!" said Delia. "I was so scared that you would be angry with me for even having been asked."

"It would have been unreasonable of me if I had been."

After that they lapsed into discussion of wedding plans. Delia wanted an early December wedding in the little church, timed so that the bells chimed just as they had their first kiss.

"Flowers will be difficult to come by, so I thought I might do pine boughs with white candles as decorations instead."

By the time it was full dark outside and Delia was ready to go home, Mary was exhausted. She bolted the door behind her friend and sank into her rocking chair. She had a lot to ponder over—the official end of her one-time dream, the revelation that she was now free to love Theodore.

The worst part of it all was her expectation when Augustus had arrived, and how foolish she had felt when he revealed his true reason for coming. She'd been so silly to think that anyone would want her—destinyless, ugly little Mary Ellmire.

She let a tear or two slide down her cheek, and then wiped them away and cleared her throat. She'd had enough self-pity for a lifetime.

Chapter Twenty

IN THE COMING WEEKS, Delia was over often to buzz over wedding plans and get Mary's advice. She was feeling an awful lot of pressure to put on the best wedding in a century, and in that way launch her flower business.

"Perhaps if I made wreaths?" she said over a mug of steaming tea, early one morning in the cottage. She'd been coming by more and more to keep Mary company. "I could have them at the wedding, and set a trend—and then people might be willing to purchase them from me! Wreaths with little red and white berries..."

Mary was able to help and advise without any thought of herself. She had put the self-pity away for good, and Delia's noble rejection of Augustus' offer had cemented Mary's adoration of her even more firmly.

It also helped that she had her own career now—one that challenged her and made her think and that left her feeling exhausted and happy at the end of the day.

On the last day of November, Alice finally invited her to come to court. Mary was so nervous that her hands shook as she dressed that morning, even though she would only have to sit and listen and try to learn something.

She met Alice very early in the morning—even before the oil lamp in the window had been lit, and they walked to the white columned building on the square that served as Tolling Bell's court and jail.

Alice took her back to her chambers, which served as her office when she was in court. Mr. Weedle, who had a thin, curled mustache, hurried in with a stack of papers and handed them silently to Alice, and then hurried out again. Mary only knew Mr. Weedle vaguely, from days in the market. She recalled that he loved strawberries, and bought them by the bushel.

"He is our clerk," said Alice, breaking the silence of the morning. Her voice sounded louder than usual in the sparsely furnished room. "He keeps the docket and helps with administrative work."

Mary had only just learned the word docket the other day —a log kept in the courtroom. "And these—" Alice hefted the stack of papers. "Are our cases for the day. Come and look."

Mary perched on a stool behind her chair and squinted down through the gloom as Alice went through each case. There were only three—though the volumes of paper would have suggested at least a dozen—and they were fairly straightforward. First they would hear a complaint from a man in a neighboring town who accused his nephew of stealing his donkey. Then a custody case, in which the mother of a child had died, and the father and grandmother were arguing over who should raise him. Finally, they would hear a complaint from the butcher that his great uncle's will had not been fairly executed.

Alice showed her how she first reviewed the case in

general, and then read each piece of evidence twice over. "I am very careful not to make any judgements at this point," she stressed to Mary. "In order to ensure justice is served, I must also ensure that every person receives a fair trial."

Mary nodded soberly. It was difficult not to form an immediate opinion, especially when she was so used to Grandma encouraging her to jump headfirst into any gut feeling she might have.

At nine thirty, Alice put on her white-powdered wig and long black robes, and led Mary into the court proper. It was an austere room, with rows of benches down each side and a podium at the front. Alice pulled a chair behind her own, so that Mary could sit slightly behind her.

The cases began at ten o'clock precisely, with everyone filing into the courtroom and settling themselves in their appointed positions.

The first case proved very trying, though not in the way Mary had expected. Both the man who swore his donkey had been stolen, and the nephew who swore he had not stolen the donkey appeared before the bench. They were dressed in their Sunday best, their hands clasped contritely behind their backs, worn shoes freshly polished.

When it was each of their turns to explain their cases, things became ridiculous. "He stole my ass!" bellowed the hunched old man, pointing at his nephew. "I saw him leading the beast away, into the field."

His nephew, in his own turn, leaned confidentially in toward them. "The old man is buggers, I tell you. He told me I could take the donkey. He isn't right in his mind! Any of them can tell you," he gestured toward their family, who was gathered in the back. "Can't even remember what he 'ad for breakfast most days, and constantly changing his mind!"

"I NEVER SAID HE COULD 'AVE MY ASS!" shouted the old man. Mary had to bite her lip not to laugh.

Alice had to bang her gavel to get things back on track. Finally, it was determined, based on testimony from his wife and children, that the old man had dementia, and had indeed told his nephew that he could borrow the donkey to move firewood.

"Those are some of my favorite cases," Alice murmured to Mary as they filed out again. "When no one really is at fault, and there's a bit of humor in it as well. The next one will be much harder."

It was harder, by far. The father of the child was a sad-eyed man with thinning black hair, and he clutched the little boy by the shoulders with nervous hands, as though terrified he would be torn away from him at any minute. He was wearing his very best clothes, but they were still shabby—the soles of his shoes worn away to almost nothing.

Mary's heart hurt just looking at them, but she knew that she couldn't form any opinions yet, and forced herself to try to think objectively.

The issue was that the father had to work full days at the mill, and wasn't able to watch his son. His grandmother—on the deceased mother's side—was a wealthy woman from Merryton, who had never approved of the match in the first place. She now wanted to take the child and bring him up as her own.

Alice heard out each party, and then leaned over her podium to look at the little boy. He shrank away from her, into his father's arms. "And what would you like?" she asked kindly.

"I want to stay with da," the boy said in a quivering voice. "I can be alone during the day, I won't get into any trouble, I swear it."

Alice sat back, looking troubled—she had explained that morning that she usually tried to carry out the child's wishes, as long as they weren't in danger and were well-loved. "Why not we try for a compromise?" she said finally. "Mrs. Townhill, would you be willing to help pay for Matthew to attend school in Merryton during the day? Then perhaps he could stop over for tea with you before coming home each day, provided he is still able to walk back in the daylight."

The old woman pursed her lips. Mary thought for a moment that she was going to refuse—it certainly was a far cry from what she had been angling for. But then her formidable shoulders slumped. The little boy's words seemed to have moved her as much as they had Mary.

"That is the best of both worlds, I suppose. But you will have to promise to study very hard, Matthew."

The little boy nodded fervently, and then ran to hug his Grandmother before sinking back into his father's arms. The father's cheeks were shiny with tears as he thanked Alice and then led his son outside into the sunshine.

"That ended well," Mary remarked once they were alone again.

"It did indeed," said Alice, her eyes crinkling. "I always go home with a lighter heart when things end happily."

The final case was very long and boring, and Mary was already exhausted from the long day. Her back ached—she kept shifting surreptitiously on the hard bench, trying to ease the pain—and her notes became brief jots of words she hadn't recognized, so that she could look them up later. A far cry from her usual diligent scribbling.

Alice though, stayed alert and crisp in her seat, listening to the proceedings with care and redirecting when necessary.

Finally, the gavel banged for the last time. Mary blinked twice, as if coming out of a long sleep. Then it was back to

Alice's chambers to review the cases and make official recordings. By the time Mary was free to walk home, she felt like a wrung out dish towel. But it was a happy sort of tired, because as exhausting as it had been, watching the cases unfold and Alice's masterful handling of each had been fascinating.

When she got home, she ate a big supper of bean soup and bread, and then went out to whisper it all to Rosie's patient, ever-listening ears. She wished she could tell Grandma—she would've loved to hear about the donkey. Mary could almost hear her bray-like laugh.

The next day she finished her sewing early—she only had one more dish towel to embroider—and set out into the woods for a walk. The sky was slate grey, and the trees nearly bare. White sycamores stuck up like skeleton hands groping for the sky.

She let her feet carry her, and soon found herself headed toward Theodore's cabin. Perhaps there was a part of her that had known where she was headed all along. She'd felt, these last few weeks, that she wasn't only mourning Grandma, but Theodore as well. She hadn't so much as glimpsed him since Grandma's funeral, and now intended to force him to face her.

But as she approached, she noticed that there was still no smoke coming from the chimney, and Sparrow's familiar "roo roo" was absent from the front porch. Had something happened? Had he gone away for good?

The cabin looked as it always did, though perhaps more closed off than usual, without the curtains open and the front door propped with a river stone.

She did a wide loop back through the woods. Her body felt very cold and empty—as though some hope had been sucked right out of her—and when she got home she couldn't even bring herself to go out to talk to Rosie. A cow was just a cow after all, even if she was a particularly empathetic one, and just now Mary craved a real, human listener. Someone who understood what she said and cried when she cried and laughed when she laughed.

Oh how she missed Grandma! If only she could have one more hour with her. Or even half an hour—to sit and talk, just as they had always used to. Mary wished that she hadn't wasted a minute of her time arguing with her—wished that from the beginning she had savored every second together. But that isn't how life, or real human relationships work, and so she had to content herself with the good times that they did have.

It didn't help that they hadn't had a Sunday dinner since the funeral. Mary had been too busy with judging and sewing, and everyone else was caught up in the business of marriage and home winterizing and work of their own.

Mary couldn't shake the empty feeling, and the frigid winter winds certainly didn't help. She felt almost worse when one Saturday afternoon she visited the little cave to fetch some apples she'd put up for the winter, and found that it was crammed full with meat.

So Theodore was still alive and well, and he'd clearly been busy this last few weeks. But it was a sure sign that he was still in town, and that he had walked right by the cottage and made no effort to contact her.

Had he somehow found out that she had feelings for him, and was hiding because he didn't return them? Her cheeks heated at even the thought of him guessing at how she felt. Worse, in his absence she couldn't ignore the thought of him that constantly lingered in the back of her mind, or the way her eyes scraped the woods to the north when she woke up each morning for signs of him.

On the second of December, Mary finally finished the

Mayor's linens. They had turned out beautifully, the embroidered cats climbing and pouncing against the white fabric. She delivered them herself, straight to his front door. He examined each napkin, dishcloth and apron with a careful eye, and then his face broke out into a great beaming grin. "They're perfect. Purrfectly perfect. She'll love them." And he fished out five whole dollars and slipped them into her hand.

Mary felt the reassurance of those folded dollars in her pocket all the way home. She'd be able to afford to live in the cottage on her own for some time with their help, and that wasn't to mention the store she already had under her mattress, or the money Grandma had left her, which she refused to so much as look at.

When she got home, the first thing that caught her eye was a cherry red cast iron pot with a lid shut tight over its contents. There had been many pots and casserole dishes left at her door since Grandma had passed, but she recognized this one immediately from the many Sunday dinners that Theo had carried it over from his cabin full of delicious food. A folded note had been stuck between the heavy lid and the pot. Heart lifting, she hefted it in her mittened hands and wedged the door open with her hip. Even through the thick wool, she could tell that it was still warm.

As soon as she'd set it down on the woodstove, she pulled her mittens off with her teeth and then snatched the note out from under the lid.

She recognized Theodore's scrawl immediately, and with her heart in her throat, read:

> *Mary,*
>
> *I hope that this finds you well. My sincere apologies for my absence these past weeks—things here have been exceedingly busy. I have been meaning to send a meal for some time—it is the neighborly thing after the passing of a loved one—so I hope that this stew feeds you well.*
>
> *—TVP*

She stood there for a moment, unable to make sense of the sharp-edged disappointment that was rising within her, choking her throat and bringing tears to her eyes. Mary couldn't have said exactly what she'd hope the note would contain, but it certainly wasn't this, with its stiff formality. Indicating that he was bringing food by because it was *neighborly*, giving no real answer for his absence...

Mary swiped angrily at the tears gathering on her cheeks and took a deep, shaky breath.

She could feel all the pieces of her life in the edges of her mind, like a great jigsaw puzzle that had yet to be assembled: her work toward becoming a judge, her love of sewing, Grandma's great big garden to manage and veggies to deliver, her Sunday mornings at church and dinners with friends, long walks through the woods. And she was content, mostly, with the makeup of them.

But if she was truly content, why was she standing here crying over a kindly delivered pot of stew?

She was beginning to believe that she wasn't meant to be happy—if anything could be meant for you when you had no destiny. Perhaps she should give it up and choose some higher cause to subscribe to instead of happiness, like justice or goodness.

But still, it would be very nice to be happy as well, if she could be.

Chapter Twenty-One

DELIA AND AUGUSTUS married on December 4th. The first snow drifted through Tolling Bell the night before, and the whole town was coated in milk-white drifts. Mary imagined that some higher power had wanted things to look especially nice for them, and so had lain snow over the town, like you might lay a white cloth over a table for special guests.

The houses were as cozy as gingerbread, with candles glimmering in the windows and boughs of evergreen on their eaves, and Mary's breath puffed out in front of her as she walked to the church that morning.

She was to be one of the bridesmaids, along with Delia's older sister, Cecilia. Delia had chosen deep burgundy gowns for them to wear, and Mary wore hers now, the heavy velvet fabric swishing pleasantly around her legs as she walked.

She met Augustus outside the church, hanging boughs of pine on the eaves. "Happy wedding day," she called to him, and he smiled down at her in a way that not even Grandma could've called primpy shrimp-ish. "Is Delia inside?"

"She's in my father's office—they're using it to get ready.

She'll be happy to see you." Mary hurried inside to the welcome warmth of the church foyer, and hung up her cloak on one of the wooden pegs in the hall. She found Delia in the office, her smile brilliant against her deep pink lips. She was already dressed in her wedding gown, an organdy as white as the snow outside.

"You look very beautiful," said Delia as she examined the bridesmaid's gown. "I knew burgundy would be a good color on you."

Mary waved the compliment away. "Look at you! You're gorgeous. Prettier than sun on the snow."

Delia spun in a circle so that her gown swung out in a graceful arc. "I do feel pretty," she admitted, presenting her profile over her shoulder—it was a sharp, handsome profile, with a strong nose and stubborn chin. "It's a good thing too, because if I didn't, I'm not sure I'd have the bravery to stand up in front of all those people and promise my life away. Now help me with my hair. Mother couldn't seem to get it right, and you have clever fingers."

Mary went to work pinning and wrapping and braiding, until Delia's hair hung in an elaborate nest on the back of her head.

"It complements your profile," said Cecilia when she came in, already dressed in her own burgundy gown. Her cloud of black hair had been captured in a gold net dotted with pearls. It was very becoming, and Mary found herself wishing that she had curls that tumbled like water over stones.

Outside in the church, guests were beginning to arrive, their shoes shiny and hair neatly coiffed. Delia and Augustus had invited the entire town, partially because he was the pastor's son and so the community all felt as though he belonged to them, and partially because Delia was hoping to impress everyone with her arrangements.

The church floor had been swept to near sparkling, and grand boughs of cedar glinted with white candles. Rose petals—imported specially—tumbled down the aisle like a foamy river, and a chandelier borrowed from Alice's house glinted above the altar. Delia had indeed made her wreaths, and they looked very graceful hung on the backs of the pews, their white and red berries bright against the dark evergreen.

Pastor Primrose stood at the door welcoming guests and directing them to their seats on either side of the pews, according to who they were more closely related to. Just as the church was beginning to fill up, Mary caught a glimpse of the back of a familiar brown tweed jacket—the same one that Theodore had worn to Grandma's funeral. Her heart leapt into her throat, and she suddenly didn't know where to look. She almost turned on her heel, to slip away into the office before he could see her.

But then Theodore turned and caught her eye, and his grin was so charmingly roguish that she was filled up to the brim with searing heat. It was the first time she'd felt warm inside since the funeral, and she pulled her arms around herself as though to simultaneously protect herself from it and trap it in.

He was seated in the front row along with the other Primrose boys, Simon and Gabriel, far from where Mary would stand with Delia.

Soon she was called back into the office, where they waited with bated breath while the music began and Augustus was brought up to the altar by his father.

"Alright," said Mrs. Trotter when their time had come, and the piano had slowed into a tinkling, sentimental song. Cecilia stepped out first, and Mary watched her walk through the double doors with her candle flickering delightfully over her face. Her nerves fluttered at the thought of tripping or spilling wax on her burgundy dress.

Then Mrs. Trotter was waving her on, and she gave Delia's hand a squeeze before walking through the doors. The lights had been dimmed, and the candles sparkled like stars in her peripheral vision.

Augustus stood at the altar, his dark suit neat against the stained-glass window behind him, face long in its solemnity. Looking at him, there was not one ounce of Mary that wished she was the one in the white gown, walking down the aisle to marry him.

She glimpsed Theodore in her peripheral vision, looking very handsome in his jacket and tie, with his beard neatly trimmed and his eyes wrinkled with emotion. Her heart missed a beat—because she knew exactly who she would like to meet at an altar—but her feet didn't falter.

As one, everyone stood to watch the bride come down the aisle. Delia was beautiful in the candlelight, her face glowing. Beside her, Augustus let out a little breath at the sight of his soon-to-be-wife.

Mary felt tears come into her eyes at the thought of that breath, but they were happy, sentimental tears, not bitter ones. She swiped them hurriedly away before Delia could see —Delia was the sort of person who always cried if you cried.

The ceremony was long—as befitted a preacher's son—but Pastor Primrose spoke sweetly and sincerely to the happiness of his son and new daughter-in-law. The audience was an appreciative one, if they weren't always attentive. And quite a few people noticed how well Mary Ellmire looked in her burgundy gown, even if she didn't have a destiny.

At the strike of noon the good pastor pronounced them man and wife, and as the bells tolled, Delia and Augustus shared their first kiss.

Afterwards, they paraded out into the church lobby, where tables had been laden with mincemeat pies and a great roast turkey and platters of jam popovers. There was an entire table devoted to dessert, which was chiefly occupied by a massive white wedding cake with sugared winter roses.

Simon Primrose was responsible for the confectionary delight—he had spent all night on it, and was looking worn but happy as he loaded his plate with the sugar cookies Mary's mother had brought. Theodore watched the festivities from a chair in the corner, his own plate balanced on his knee. Occasionally they would exchange smiles as Mary was whisked from one duty to another. She longed to go over and speak to him, but was feeling suddenly shy, and was almost glad for the endless litany of things Delia needed from her.

She fetched speeches for uncles and sopped up spills near the drink table and fixed Delia's hair when it started to come undone. When finally she had a free moment to stop and catch her breath, she looked up to find that Theodore had disappeared.

The warmth in her breast started to slip away again—she had hoped he'd approach her, perhaps even walk her home. Mary was glad when at last they sent the happy couple off to their new little apartment above the tailor's shop. Now she could clean up in peace, with only the minimal word here and there to determine who was doing what.

Word had spread rapidly that Delia's destiny was to be a florist, and so the people of Tolling Bell had come to the wedding ready to judge her floral choices as a professional. But they'd left touched by the true emotion behind every detail, and soon forgot to think of her destiny at all and enjoyed the day for what it was instead.

Which perhaps wasn't good for Delia's business, but it

was much better luck for a budding marriage to be taken as a couple in love than an advertisement.

When the food had been stowed, the tables wiped clean and the chandelier returned to Alice's house, Mary was free to go home at last.

She felt even more exhausted than she had after her day at court—as though she had been holding her emotions under a looking glass all day, waiting for the faintest hint of jealousy so that she could obliterate it.

But it hadn't showed. Instead, all she felt was mystified by Theodore's odd behavior, and empty and cold again since he'd disappeared. Now she wanted to go home and curl up under Grandma's thickest blanket and take a nap.

She made sure to give Rosie a good brushing and milking, and told her all about the wedding. And she put the chickens safely away in the coop and latched it firmly closed—it was the time of year when prey was scarce for the wild things of the land—but then she marched right inside and stepped gratefully out of that constricting burgundy gown. In that moment, she felt that there was no greater pleasure than to curl up in a comfortable spot under a warm blanket, sip a mug of tea, and not think about the plagues of life.

The next week provided a welcome break to the little village of Tolling Bell. The snow that had started on Delia and Augustus's wedding day continued through the week, until they were so laden with it that travel was impossible.

It was all Mary could do to create a path to the paddock and woodpile so that she could feed the chickens and Rosie and fetch wood for the fire. She stressed and stressed about the snow on the roof—it was growing alarmingly high. Last year Mr. Templeton's entire house had collapsed in a similar snowstorm. She even endeavored to clear it herself, but she had never cleared a roof before, and Grandma only had a rickety wooden ladder that required two people to keep stable.

When it had almost reached the barren branches of the oak tree above, Mary resolved that she'd ask her father to come out and clear it the next day, little as she liked the idea of asking for help.

But help appeared on its own. The next morning she came home from her weekly breakfast with Delia to find that it had been mysteriously cleared.

Breakfast had been especially pleasant—Delia was excited to share about her new married life, and Mary was curious to hear. She'd never had a married friend before, and the idea of living with a man aside from her father was foreign to her. She thought she'd enjoy it, except for the beard hairs in the sink that Delia described, and the muddy boots.

It had been equally fun to sit in the little apartment Pastor Primrose had rented for them until he was ready to retire from the parsonage. Delia served tea in her very own china, and they sat and sipped by the window and felt very grown up. Down below, two younger girls held hands and spun in the snow, while a third little girl watched, large dark eyes cautious. Mary smiled fondly, looking at her.

Delia caught her gaze and looked down on them as well. "It feels like lifetimes since we were that little."

"It does," Mary agreed. "Though I'm very glad to have finally grown up."

Afterwards Mary walked home whistling, imagining how she would arrange her own little house if she had the chance, when she noticed straightaway that the tin roof glinted through the trees in the bright snow light.

The snow was now piled neatly at the side of the house, so that it overlapped with Grandma's bedroom window.

There was no note, and the only clue as to who had done

it could be found by a set of boot prints that had tromped through the snow from the woods along the lake and back again—though whether it was Simon or Theodore, Mary could not determine.

Regardless, she was grateful, and thanked her lucky stars for kindly neighbors who kept an eye on her. The next day she set out toward the cabins on the lake to get a glimpse of them (and to try to determine if Theodore was indeed home again).

As she got close, she realized that he was outside, hammering away at something on the side of his house. She felt suddenly too shy to come closer—it had been so long since they had really spoken—and instead veered around his cabin to find Simon.

He was drinking tea on his deepset porch, wrapped in a thick layer of blankets. Mary noted that his own roof was towering with snow.

"You might want to clear that," she said, nodding up at it. "It could collapse your house."

Simon laughed, seeming cheered by the idea instead of discouraged by it. "If it were to happen to anyone it'd be me, wouldn't it? Lord knows this house isn't as sturdy as it could be."

He hopped up to lean over the wobbly porch rail and survey the pile of snow. For a long moment they both gazed at it, eyes half blinded by the shine of sun, and then Simon regarded her. "That can't be what you came for though, can it? Would you like tea or some such?"

"No thank you," she said after a moment of consideration. "I was just on a tromp and figured I'd see if you were the mysterious person who cleared my roof."

He laughed again. "Clearly not me. If you find the person who did, send them my way!"

"I most certainly will," said Mary with a grin. And with a few more pleasantries, Mary set off again into the winter wonderland, reflecting that if she couldn't have a life partner, at least she had very good friends.

Chapter Twenty-Two

SEVERAL WEEKS WENT BY, and every once in a while Mary would catch a glimpse of Theodore, working away at his house. First it was banging and hammering, and then he'd installed two flower boxes on the front windows. The next time she peered through the woods at it, there was a second rocker on his porch.

Mary wasn't sure what to make of these changes—it seemed an odd time of year to be concerned about making home repairs, but Theodore had never cleaved to convention. She'd also seen him trekking to market each week, pulling a red wooden sled loaded with meat.

Usually he only went to market once a month—as she'd overheard him explain it to Grandma one afternoon last summer, his expenses were small and he only needed the money from his hunting to purchase necessaries like flour and sugar.

Unlike Grandma, he had no cow to feed—his goats would eat anything off the land they could find. He had all the books he could read, and a library to borrow from when he needed something new. All the rest he could trade for.

Mary loved the idea of that sort of self-sufficiency. He had only as much as he needed and no more. How different than the life she had grown up in, with a house full of antiques and useless decor that constantly required dusting, and where people gave each other useless, cluttering items at every opportunity.

Inspired, she swore to herself that she wouldn't let herself be one of those people. For this Christmas, she would give only presents that people needed or could enjoy right off— and Christmas was drawing near, so she had an opportunity to test her new resolution.

The next market day she went into town to see about useful, wanted presents. Theodore's booth was conspicuously absent. Mary's eyes had gone right to the spot where it always stood as soon as she'd arrived, and she'd had to tamp down her disappointment at his absence.

It was odd that he was gone, when he had been coming so consistently. She stopped by Simon's booth, which was laden with snow-white cupcakes, with small snow men piped out of icing on top of them, and a pile of white-packaged meat. "I'm selling both baked goods and meat today," said Simon cheerfully. "I'm a regular one-stop shop. Theodore has gone over to Merryville for the day."

"What's he gone to Merryville for?" She asked, trying not to look too intensely interested.

Simon shrugged. "He didn't say—he was rather mysterious about the whole business."

Mary frowned. "Well, I hope he's all right," she said finally. Merryville was known for having some of the best doctors in the region.

Having heard the news she'd hoped to hear, Mary excused herself and continued on through the market. She wondered what he was doing so far from home—she had never heard of him leaving before.

She shook the matter from her mind—it wasn't any of her business, anyway—and set to present purchasing. For Delia she planned to embroider new linens—she had none for her house yet, and Mary could sew the latest styles for her. For her parents she purchased miniature, golden jars of honey—both her parents had a ferocious sweet tooth. For Alice she bought a bottle of port—it certainly wouldn't last long enough to clutter her house. And for Simon she purchased a carved wooden cake stand that would look splendid in the main window of the bakery.

A red plaid hat lined with rabbit fur caught her eye at Mr. Bright's booth. It brought Theodore instantly to mind—or perhaps it was that he was always on her mind these days. She had seen him several mornings with nothing but a holey knit hat pulled on over his ears, and now she stood for some time fingering the soft fur, debating whether or not she should purchase it.

It seemed very odd to get a present for someone who had avoided you for weeks. But then Mr. Bright tucked his chin to his chest and said, "Well?" impatiently, and Mary fished out seventy-five cents then and there and bought it. At the very least, she reflected as she walked home with her goodies, she could wear it to milk the cow in the mornings.

With a week till Christmas, Mary decided something had to be done about the cottage. It had become very gloomy in Grandma's absence—while she'd hung up one of the wreaths from Delia's wedding on the front door, there were no longer fresh things in vases inside or cheery candles in the windows, and with the long winter nights it was getting to be downright depressing.

In her parents' house she knew they would be putting

mistletoe up in the doorway, baking constant mounds of sugar cookies, and singing off-key carols night and day, which was cozy certainly, but wasn't her way. She wanted something more serene and less sweet for her own tradition.

So she purchased tallow from the butcher and made her own candles, scented with pine sap from the surrounding trees, and with Delia's help cut big armfuls of white pine to make garlands for each of their homes. They spent the entirety of a Saturday crimping boughs of evergreen to wire, and then wrapping it around Mary's stair, pausing regularly to munch on the biscuits Delia had brought from Simon's bakery.

Delia was just donning her cloak when there was a rap on the door. They both looked up, and Delia smiled slyly at Mary.

"Have you been seeing Theodore much these days?"

"I haven't," Mary said faintly, but she crossed to the door in two large strides.

Outside, Augustus Primrose stood, his cap in his hands, smiling sheepishly at her. Mary did her best to banish a sudden sense of crossness—it was the second time she'd been disappointed by Augustus at the door.

"I missed my wife," he said by way of explanation. "And as the sun was setting, I thought she might fancy a hand to hold on the way home."

Delia could hardly hide her incandescent happiness. It glowed in the burnished bronze of her cheeks, and lit up her eyes. Mary gave her a hug goodbye, and then waved the couple off, lingering in the doorway for a moment to watch them disappear into the snowy forest, mittened hands clasped, Augustus pulling a bright blue sled piled high with garland with his free hand.

Internally, she was wrestling with a deep longing that had

sprung up within her at the scene—Augustus's sweet shyness, Delia's obvious joy, the intimate way she leaned her head against his shoulder as they walked.

When they'd disappeared into the lengthening shadows, she closed the door and surveyed the cottage. It did seem cheerier with the candles flickering and the cozy garland. But loneliness lurked in the shadows.

Mary missed Grandma terribly. She kept waiting for the longing to cease, but it only seemed to grow with each new thing she wished to tell her, each funny or happy memory. The missing was worst at night, when memories of lying in bed with Grandma during thunderstorms, pressed in so close to her that they lay cheek to cheek, brought the tears flooding back. She felt as though she'd gone her whole life without really being understood, and then she'd finally found someone who understood the good and the bad of her, and even better—loved her for it all—and then she'd lost her.

She only felt lonelier as the days ticked nearer to Christmas, heightened by the cheerfully snowy, lantern-lit streets in town, with mittened couples holding hands on every corner. She found herself eyeing the sleek, fat cats that curled in the windows of houses. Perhaps a cat would help her loneliness. Then at least she wouldn't be the only living being inside.

At two weeks until Christmas, Mary was interrupted from working on Delia's Christmas present by a knock on the door. Court had been cancelled that day thanks to a fresh dumping of snow, and so Mary had taken the opportunity to curl up by the fireplace under Grandma's thickest red blanket.

She opened the door without much expectation and promptly dropped her sewing. Theodore stood outside in a brilliant beam of sunshine. He was smiling, but his cheeks looked tight, and his hands were white-knuckled at his sides—

they reminded her of Augustus's hands when he'd stood outside to ask her blessing to marry Delia.

He was alone—he looked very odd without the little red dog at his side.

"Theodore," she said, stooping quickly to recover her sewing so that she wouldn't have to meet his eyes.

"Mary," he said. Just hearing her name on his tongue made her stomach do awful somersaults. "I've come to ask you to go on an adventure with me."

The way he said it was oddly formal—much more formal than she'd ever heard him be in the past. And now that she looked more closely at him, she saw that he was dressed rather too nicely for an adventure—in a thick woolen grey sweater pulled over a dress shirt, and pressed pants. Even his boots had been shined, and his beard had been trimmed back to tidiness.

His head, she noticed, was bare. His straight brown hair stuck up from his widow's peak as though he'd only just run his fingers nervously through it. She'd have to give him that hat after all.

"I—certainly," she managed to get out. The thought crossed her mind to refuse him. There was a part of her that was still cross with him for disappearing when she needed him most. But all the rest of her jumped immediately at the chance to spend time with him again, and for the opportunity to resolve the mystery of where he'd been.

"What sort of adventure?" she asked as an afterthought, already pulling on her boots and cloak.

"To get a Christmas tree," he said, and flashed her a more genuine smile. "It was a tradition between your Grandma and myself. She had an eye for bushy, well-rounded ones, and I'm adept at cutting them down and dragging them home." He gestured to the hatchet looped onto his sleek brown dress belt.

"Aren't you dressed rather nicely for cutting down trees?"

He laughed, but it was a nervous laugh, and he didn't answer otherwise.

Mary had never had a Christmas tree before. Pastor Primrose insisted they were a pagan tradition and belonged to heathens and not Christians, so her parents had always stuck to wreaths and stockings.

But she had always dearly loved the idea of bringing a tree in the house and decorating it. At last she would have the chance.

Theodore was silent as they walked toward the opposite side of the lake, where a stand of spruce spread their needles over the ground like a carpet. Mary cast careful looks at his face as they walked, and was alarmed to see that he looked very stern, his brow furrowed as though he were in deep concentration.

Perhaps he had invited her out of obligation toward Grandma, she wondered. Or because he felt sorry for her. The second thought made her feel ashamed, and she almost wished she hadn't come.

When they reached the spruce stand his face opened up again like the sun coming out from behind clouds. He'd point out a tree, laden with snow and dotted with miniature pinecones like it had been ornamented already, and Mary would shake her head and point out a bare spot on the rear side or a bird's nest in the top branches.

It was very beautiful beneath the great, snowy boughs. Occasional clumps of snow would drift to the ground, and the whole world was muffled and soft and glistening. Ice coated the hardwoods so that they looked as though a painter had come through with his brush and painstakingly applied lacquer to every bare branch.

Their banter loosened as they argued over the merits of

different trees. Mary was far from an expert, having never picked out a Christmas tree before, but she was very good at forming opinions about things. Soon she had a list of criteria to judge each tree by.

Theodore had a fondness for scraggly, crooked trees. Mary made him laugh with her eagerness in pointing out their flaws. She'd say, "It has two points on top, how will you choose which to put a star on?" or "I suppose that one is nice, if you like shrubs," and his laughter would boom out through the still woods.

Just as their faces were starting to stiffen with cold, they climbed a gentle slope and came to a stop beside a spruce with close-growing, snow heavy branches. Its bark was a deep,

beautiful red against the green and white forest. They slipped beneath the snowy branches and were encased in what felt like a private, separate room of the woods—the ground was bare of snow here, and red pine needles coated the ground beneath their feet.

Neither said anything for a moment. Something about this tree felt right, even though it was largely the same as many dozen others they had set eyes on. Mary had a sudden sense of something building between them, and for the first time she looked up into those kindly brown eyes.

He was very close—there wasn't much room beneath the tree. All Mary had to do was reach up several inches, and she'd be able to skim her fingers along the line of his jaw. As though he knew what she was thinking, his jaw tensed.

"Mary—" he began, and her stomach flipped, "when I asked you to go on an adventure today, I only told you about the smallest part of what I had in mind."

"What do you mean?" she asked, the skin pinching between her eyes. Did he mean a longer hike into the woods? She was getting cold, and wasn't sure how much longer she wanted to be out, especially if they had to cut and drag two Christmas trees inside.

Theodore sank onto one knee, and took her cold little hands in his own great big warm ones. Suddenly Mary's stomach wasn't doing singular flips, but a series of somersaults, in time with the pounding of her heart.

"I mean that I love you." It was hard for Mary to catch the flow of his words over the roaring in her head. "That I'd like to live my life alongside you. I've known for a long time now that you are exceptionally dear to me—and more so, that you challenge and enchant me. But it wasn't until the day of Grandma Isabella's funeral, when I saw you in the field of goldenrod, so gleeful and golden and alive, that I knew you were my woman in yellow."

He took a deep breath and went on, a little less certainly now. "If you don't feel the same way about me I understand, of course. I'll respect your wishes whatever they are, but I do hope—Oh—" he smiled weakly, and then let go of Mary's hands to fumble in his pocket, "and I almost forgot, I've got a ring and everything." At last, he pulled out a black velvet box.

Inside was a gem as white and sparkling as the snow, in a setting beside two stones the same deep green as the needles of the tree they stood beneath. It wasn't only Mary's face that was numb now, she couldn't feel her legs.

"I should probably ask the question, shouldn't I? I'm making an awful mess of this—I've never been so nervous in my life." He took a deep, steadying breath, and then went on. "Mary Eloise Moore Ellmire, will you marry me?"

"I—I," Mary struggled to make her tongue move. "Yes, of course I will! Only I can't believe it!"

Theodore's face twisted with happiness. "Believe it!" he commanded, and pulled her to him. His lips were warm on hers, and his beard was much softer on her face than she had imagined it would be. Her whole body came alive again at his touch, and any numbness or disbelief she felt was banished wholly.

When they'd come back to themselves, Theodore very carefully slid the ring onto her finger.

There was still one last thing on Mary's mind though, before she could feel perfectly happy. "Theodore," she began hesitantly, "Why did you disappear for so long after Grandma's funeral, if you knew you loved me then?"

Theodore shook his head ruefully. "It was silly, to be honest, and doesn't reflect well on my character. I knew that as soon as I saw you alone again, I would blurt out all of my feelings. But I didn't have enough money for a ring, and I wanted to do the thing properly. So I headed out into the woods, to hunt and fish as much as I could. It was a miserable time—cold and damp, with no real joy in being out when I knew you must be sad and hurting at home. And then—well, my house wasn't fit for a wife, let alone children—" Mary could barely breathe for the swell of happiness that rose up through her breastbone at the thought of their own little baby, "—so I had repairs to make so that it might be good enough for you."

"I love your cabin, and I would've loved it even without the repairs," said Mary. "But it will be hard to leave Grandma's cottage behind."

"I thought about that," said Theo in a rush. "It is smaller than mine, but perhaps we could expand it—I could add on a second bedroom. And I'd need to expand the paddock for the goats."

"That sounds perfect," said Mary. "And in the meantime, we can live in your cottage."

That settled, they ducked back under the snowy branches to find a Christmas tree. It didn't take long—Theo pointed out a scraggly little tree that was exactly to his liking. Mary was too blinded by happiness to see any flaws in it at all.

"We'll be sharing a house soon," said Theodore as he balanced it on his shoulder after he'd chopped it down. "So I think one tree should do."

Mary laughed at the sheer delightfulness of the idea. "How soon would you like to be married?"

"As soon as possible, I should think. I'm done with waiting, and I don't care much for a large wedding."

"Nor do I," said Mary. "Perhaps we could marry at the courthouse, with Alice as our officiant."

Theodore beamed at the idea. "That seems perfectly fitting for the two of us. None of that blathering on that my father does. And after we can have a Sunday-style dinner, with everyone pitching in for food and drink, and celebrating properly."

As they neared Theodore's cabin, Mary's eyes settled on the window boxes, now full of snow. The cabin was tucked cozily into the pines, and a plume of smoke rose from the chimney. Through the window, she could see Sparrow dancing joyfully, waving her banner of a tail in welcome. Another wave of sheer happiness washed over her, so powerful that she nearly swayed on her feet. Soon, this cozy scene would be hers, too. She could hardly believe how very wonderful her life had suddenly become.

Chapter Twenty-Three

Mary looked around the little cottage. She loved the little stone fireplace, crackling merrily, with the two great sofas bellied up to it. A braided rug upon the flagstones made the room downright cozy. At the far side of the room, a green-painted door opened to a small bedroom.

A big, pot-bellied stove dominated the kitchen, a cast iron teapot perched on top. In the window over the sink, Theo had planted herbs in tiny pots, and they pressed their leaves against the glass in search of sunlight. Built in shelves were piled with novels and cookbooks and plant identification manuals, and his earthenware crockery was set out to good display on either side of the sink.

She would have to bring some of Grandma's pillows and blankets for the sofa, but otherwise it was just about perfect.

"I'll wait to give you a tour of the bedroom," said Theo. His cheeks flushed and he rubbed at the nape of his neck. "But you're welcome to peek up if you'd like." He gestured to a ladder that disappeared into a loft obscured from the ground floor by slotted railing.

Mary climbed several rungs upward, until she could see

above the wooden floorboards to the bedroom above. A tidy full bed pressed up against a large window, out of which the woods could be seen. The thick forest green knit blanket—Mary recognized Grandma's work—was draped over what appeared to be a fraying patchwork quilt. A black cat was curled in a ball on one of the pillows, and it blinked sleepy eyes at Mary before twitching its tail.

And in the peak of the window, a heavy, iron wrought lantern hung, shining out a bright warm light through the glass. Mary flushed to see it—knowing that it was the same light she'd first seen through her own bedroom window. And to think that it'd been hanging up above Theo's head at night all these months, mere feet from where he slept!

From the loft you could see the fireplace below, and half of one of the couches, and from the front window could just catch a glimpse of the gleaming lake.

It was a cozy, comfortable little room, and Mary could see herself sleeping soundly and

happily there. "Where does Sparrow sleep?" she asked as she descended.

"She stays down here on the sofa. The ladder is too steep for her." Theo was busy putting the tree's trunk into a large, earthenware pot, and then propping it upright with planks of wood. Mary moved automatically to help hold the tree upright. "Thanks." He smiled up at her, and Mary felt another wave of happy disbelief that he was to be her husband.

When the tree was upright, he produced a number of ornaments from a tin box he pulled out of the back of a closet. There was a miniature red clay dog reminiscent of Sparrow, several shiny gold balls, and a number of pinecones.

"My mother gave me this one the year before she passed," he said, holding up a glass ornament in the shape of an icicle.

It glimmered fragilely in the firelight as he hung it carefully at the very front of the tree. "We never had a tree indoors when I was growing up, as my father said it was a heathen tradition, but Ma loved to decorate the little pine tree outside the parsonage..."

His voice trailed off, and Mary reached up to squeeze his hand, still marveling that it was her right to do so. That he was *hers* to comfort and love and hold.

After a moment, he cleared his throat, and produced strings of popcorn and cranberries, and showed her how to wrap them evenly around.

"I usually go out on Christmas day and put up some of these strings on outdoor trees as well, in her honor," Theo told her as he stepped back to admire the effect. "That way all the critters in the land can have a treat."

"We'll have to do it this year as well," Mary said, cottoning to the idea as soon as he'd said it. It seemed right to give something to the land, when it gave them so much.

When at last the tree had been decorated, Theodore and Sparrow walked her home. He gave her another lingering kiss on the doorway, and then Mary watched him disappear into the woods.

As soon as he was gone, she dashed to the paddock to tell Rosie everything. More than ever, she wished Grandma were here. She couldn't imagine news that would make Grandma happier. But it was good to tell Rosie's patient ears, and to stroke her warm muzzle.

That night, Rosie was the only one to hear the news. Mary wanted to hug it privately to herself for a little longer. She went to bed thinking that at last she'd found her missing puzzle piece, and that her life might now be happy as well as good.

THE NEXT DAY, Alice noticed the ring on her finger almost immediately. It was to be a reading and studying day in Alice's office, and Mary had no sooner picked up the list of vocabulary words and concepts off of the desk when Alice snatched her hand up for inspection.

"You have news, miss!" she said with keen excitement.

Mary grinned. She had been excited to tell Alice, because she knew the woman would be almost as joyous as Grandma might have been. Soon the entire story had been told, from beginning to end.

Alice clasped her hands in front of her face. "My cheeks hurt from grinning," she said. "I'd be honored to marry the two of you. There's no more fitting wedding for a judge than one in a courtroom. It's where Sadie and I were married, back when we were young things. It's only too bad Grandma Isabella can't be with us."

"I've been missing her more than ever lately," agreed Mary. "It's odd to feel both so very happy and so very sad all at once."

After her lessons were over, Mary walked over to her parents' house to share the news. They were understandably gobsmacked. Their prim, proper daughter was to marry one of the worst scoundrels in the town, and she was positively glowing over it.

But they pulled themselves together and gave her their blessing, and wished only that the pair might have a happy life together. It helped that they remembered his tears at Grandma's funeral—no one truly horrible could cry like that at a little old woman's burial.

Before she left, Mary turned and said over her shoulder,

"And you might want to ask Theodore the true story of how his dog lost her leg. It might redeem him for you."

When she was gone, they decided they would most certainly do that, and that while Theodore wasn't who they would have picked for their daughter, they were happy she'd found anyone who wanted to marry her at all.

The last stop she made was to see Delia and Augustus in their little apartment on the square. "It seems the second half of your destiny held true for both of us," she said by way of breaking the news. "I too will marry the Primrose boy I least expected."

Delia clapped a hand over her mouth, and screamed shrilly and happily into it, while Augustus patted Mary tentatively on the back. "Theodore, I presume?" said Augustus. "I've wondered for some time when he would ask. It's been a long time since I saw him as happy as he's been this last year."

"I had no idea," said Mary honestly. "But I'm very happy that's the case." Delia broke out a bottle of wine—their wedding gift from Alice—and poured it out into their brand new glasses.

Delia and Mary held them up in celebration and then downed the warming juice in one big gulp, while Augustus managed to both frown disapprovingly and smile at the same time.

"I'm afraid it will be a small wedding," she said to Delia, "so there won't be any flowers needed."

"That's alright, dear. A small wedding suits you."

After that she took her leave of them and went home to find that she had guests waiting in her kitchen—Theodore, Simon, and the Primrose boy she knew least well, Gabriel. Simon gave her a great, rib cracking hug while Theodore beamed.

Gabriel gave Mary a shy hug and a smile, and Mary

caught a glint in his eye that told her that she'd come to love this Primrose as much as she did the rest of the family. When at last they'd departed, Mary sat in stunned, happy silence in Grandma's rocking chair. In the span of one happy day, her dearest friend had become her fiancé, and his whole, wonderful family would be hers too.

Since Grandma's death she had felt awfully alone in the world—she'd had only two parents who didn't understand her well—but now she would have an entire family to love and care for.

Mary didn't know it, but around town the news was spreading faster than the common cold. That prim, proper, Mary Ellmire should marry someone like Theodore Primrose was mind boggling to the people of Tolling Bell.

The less kind people chalked it up to her being destinyless and desperate for a husband (Mrs. Dennison happily spread this version of the rumor), but anyone with any humor at all enjoyed the match greatly. "It'll breathe life into the girl, and bring the boy back to earth," they said amongst themselves.

Theodore and Mary chose a day to be married—the Saturday before Christmas, and after that the arrangements quickly came to shape. Theodore would be married in his brown tweed jacket, and Mary sewed a new dress—one the palest shade of yellow she could find, the color of creamy summer butter. It seemed only fitting that Theo's wife be married in yellow.

Delia braided sprigs of spruce into a crown to be worn in her hair, and a belt of spruce to go around her waist.

The courtroom was reserved for the day, Alice was officially recruited to marry them, and all of their nearest and dearest friends were notified of the date and time.

They kept the decorations simple—no chandeliers for

them—but Delia insisted they at least line the aisle with spruce boughs and candles.

Looking into the mirror on the day of her wedding, Mary could hardly believe she was the same person she had been a year ago. She could still feel the thread of self that connected her to her past—that moral little person who cared so much about rules and doing right and living properly. And she was glad to still feel it. It is a disconcerting thing to feel completely disconnected from one's past self.

But she had grown so much—her dreams had become so much bigger and braver, her smile so much more honest. She beamed at herself in the mirror, and felt beautiful and happy and young. Behind her, Delia smiled with her, and her mother marveled at how she had transformed from a dowdy old maid to a beautiful young woman in so short a span of time.

She felt terribly nervous when it was time to walk down the aisle, but because of Grandma she knew that it was only a sign that she was challenging herself and growing. Then the doors opened, and she saw Theodore waiting for her at the end of the aisle, his eyes crinkled in a smile, so very handsome in his jacket and crisp white shirt, and the nerves disappeared altogether.

Theodore and Mary had decided to stand alone at the altar, aside from Alice, and so the rest of their relatives and friends were seated on the wooden benches of the courtroom. All their faces turned toward her, and they were smiling, and her mother was crying, and Mary felt such a great swell of warmth and appreciation for them all that she thought she might lift off of the ground. Even Sparrow was there, her tongue out and smiling, wearing her a garland of her own around her neck.

The only person missing was Grandma, but they left a

seat in the front row open for her, and Simon even laid her pipe upon a cushion. So she was there in spirit.

Then Mary was up at the altar, and Theodore had taken her hands in his, and Alice was speaking words that Mary could only hear through a thick cloud of happiness that seemed to have separated her and Theodore from the world. She was reminded of standing under the spruce tree with him, in their own private room in the woods.

Before she knew it, she had murmured "I do," and Theodore had said "I do," in his confident baritone and then they were allowed to kiss.

That kiss didn't hold a candle to their first under the spruce tree, but it was firm and warm and it held steadiness instead of passion, which in ways is more important, because passion wanes, but steadiness holds on forever.

Mary and Theodore both cried as they walked back down the aisle together, blurring their guests into whirls of fantastic color.

"We would've made Grandma the happiest person in the world today," Theo said, and they both fell silent for a few beats, thinking of all she might have said. Their solemnity was soon broken though, because their guests were coming out of the courtroom, and hugs and kisses had to be exchanged all around. Then they all trooped through the snow, back to the cabin, where he lifted her over the threshold to great cheers, and then they all stormed in and got started with the celebrating.

Their friends and family had gone all out in their culinary preparations. Simon had baked a lemon meringue to rival the one he had made last summer—it towered above the other dishes, decorated in candied lemons and sugared goldenrod. Pastor Primrose and Gabriel had brought a giant stack of custard popovers, Alice filled the beverages counter with bottle after dusty bottle of warming port and cider.

Theodore had roasted a great haunch of venison with dates and prunes and spicy dried chiles into a stew, and it was warm and sweet and rich in the crisp winter air. Her mother brought her famous sugar cookies, and her father brought spicy smelling cedar wood to burn in the fire. Delia brought a platter of caramelized carrots she'd dug up from her cellar.

Even Rosie was included—Simon led her up onto the porch, so that she could look in through the window and be part of the festivities, and Sparrow happily trotted from person to person, collecting pats and ear scratches.

After a big earthenware mug of port, several bowls of stew, and a slice of meringue, Mary was left warm and content. She sat with Theodore on the sofa, his arm tucked snugly around her, and her whole body full with sleepy happiness.

She fell asleep that way, unaware of the revelry going on around her, or that her new husband looked down with such tenderness that the hearts of the entire party were touched.

Even Pastor Primrose found that he couldn't doubt the happiness of their marriage, even if Mary didn't have a destiny. There was something about the girl that was wise beyond her years—wise beyond the primness and properness that sometimes seemed to be her sole personality trait. And she certainly made his son happy.

At sundown they crept away, and Mary awoke to find herself alone with her new husband. For a moment she was disoriented, but then she looked out the window at the sun setting in brilliant pink flames over the lake. Theodore's face was lit by the sunshine streaming inside, and she remembered everything and felt supremely glad to wake up and find it was still reality.

Her father had delivered her trunk with all of her things to the bedroom upstairs, and that morning Theodore and Simon had helped shut down Grandma's cottage for the rest of the winter and get Rosie settled in her new paddock.

Mary looked around with bemused, sleepy eyes, and her gaze settled on the black cat, who was hanging over the back of a chair like a great panther. "What's the cat's name?" she asked. It was a matter she'd been wondering about for some time now, but kept forgetting to ask.

"Lucifer," said Theodore, and the cat's tail twitched. "Because he's a devil. You two will have to come to terms with each other, and I fear it will take some time. He isn't one for change, and he likes to make mischief."

As if he knew they were talking about him, Lucifer gave a great stretch and jumped down from the back of the chair to pad lazily over. He rubbed politely against Mary's ankles, swatted at Theo's socked foot with his claws out, and then stalked toward the kitchen.

Mary laughed. "I see what you mean."

"You'll have to get used to me as well, I fear," Theo said, and swept her up into another kiss—this one with so much passion that she forgot to measure it against the others at all.

Chapter Twenty-Four

THE DAY after their wedding was Christmas Eve. He woke her in the middle of the night, and they snowshoed out through fresh powder. It was a full moon, and the light gleamed subtly on every bough and icy leaf. Sparrow joined them and leapt gleefully through shadows and moonbeams.

Mary couldn't imagine a better way to celebrate Christmas's coming. The next day they had a quiet, sleepy morning by their tree, drinking coffee and reflecting on how rich and happy their lives had become in so short a time.

Theo gave her a canvas pack of her own, so that she could join him on overnight expeditions, and Mary gave him his hat. He was delighted with it, and immediately pulled it on to keep his ears warm against the morning chill.

They spent the afternoon out in the woods, looking for their spruce tree so that they might decorate it for the birds and squirrels. It took some doing to find, but then Mary found the little rise in the ground, and her feet brought her to the tree quite naturally.

Theodore undid his strings of cranberries and popcorn, and they draped them over the tree boughs. It made a very beautiful picture in the fading light—the red of the cranberries and white of the popcorn on the deep, glorious green.

Mary couldn't stop gazing at Theodore, entranced by the rich textures of his beard and handknit sweater, and then he looked back at her, and she flushed so prettily that he had no choice but to sweep her into his arms for a kiss.

That evening they went around to their families' homes and distributed presents, their faces lit by the lanterns they carried with them. Mary kept her hand clasped in Theo's—she felt that as long as she could hold his hand, she could bear the cold all night.

It was a pleasure to come back through the woods, and see their candles shining in the windows of the little cabin. Inside was blessedly warm. They took off their heavy layers of coats and gloves and hats and scarves, and snuggled up on the floor next to the fire with mugs of tea and a book each.

IN THE COMING WEEKS, Mary found that life as a married woman was much to her liking. It was sheer bliss to wake up to Theo's beloved face each morning, after they'd stayed up late the night before talking until the oil burned low in the lamp.

They'd rise early together, and Mary would go out to milk Rosie while Theo chopped wood for the fireplace. Then they'd come back together, flushed with cold and exertion, and they'd have a breakfast of porridge. Theo drank his coffee as rich black sludge. At first Mary couldn't stomach it, but she found that if she added a bit of cream, skimmed off of the morning's milk, it became very palatable.

Theodore's tradition was to sit out on the porch with his

coffee regardless of the weather, so Mary joined him, and she came to love watching the sun glimmer on the frozen lake as she wrapped her hands tight around the warmth of her mug. He'd even make her a nest of blankets in her rocker so that she didn't get chilled.

"Aren't you afraid to damage your eyes?" she asked one particularly bright morning, as Theo gazed into the sunrise.

He laughed, eyes crinkling in the warm yellow light. "Why bother having eyes, if it isn't to look at beautiful things?"

On working days sometimes he'd rise well before the sun, and creep off into the woods with his bow slung over his shoulder. Mary would get up alone to watch the sunrise reflected on the ice before she hiked into town to have her lessons with Alice.

When she came home, Theodore would be back, sometimes cleaning an animal, other times waiting for her on the porch with Sparrow, his great black pipe sticking out between his teeth.

The nights, which had been so long and lonely in Grandma's cottage, were cozy with Theodore. He always had a new book to read, and sometimes he would lie on his back on the sofa and read aloud to her, while she knitted or sewed, or merely stared absently into the fire, his voice richer and smoother than port.

When they grew sleepy, they would rinse their mugs in the sink and climb up the ladder to the cozy bed waiting for them. Theodore was like a furnace in the night, and he'd wrap his arms around her so that she never had to wait for the sheets to warm up before she was comfortable.

Lucifer often slept at their feet, like a furry hot water bottle, purring into his whiskers. Sparrow curled up on the couch cushion closest to the fire below, and they would all slip into dreams of moonlight and snow and ice.

On the coldest mornings, Mary woke before Theodore, and lay silently in his arms, not wanting him to wake and rise. It was so perfectly warm beneath their covers, so wonderfully satisfying to lie together, that she never wanted those mornings to end.

January slipped quickly into February, and the endless snows began to let up, replaced by icy winds that raced across the lake and buffeted the cabin. Mary didn't mind the wind—it only made their cabin cozier.

Soon even February had passed, and March brought with it warmer days. The icicles on the porch began to drip and shrink, while a giant puddle of water formed in the middle of the lake, and great chunks of ice drifted like icebergs through the clear patches of water.

"This summer I'll teach you to canoe and swim," Theo told her one morning as they watched Sparrow dip her paws in the icy water. "We'll have to get you one of those scandalous little bathing suits, and we can spend long afternoons on the water, fishing and swimming and picnicking."

In the meantime, wild thunderstorms shook the earth, and kept Mary and Theodore huddled up together in their cabin while rain pelted the tin roof and streamed down the windows. Usually the spring rains left Mary feeling cooped up and impatient for summer, but there was something so romantic and cozy about lying on the couch with her feet draped over Theodore's lap, napping the afternoon away, or starting on a new adventure story, that this year she didn't mind. In fact, she was sad when the rains let up, and they had to rejoin the world.

April arrived, and still Mary couldn't imagine being happier. Of course, not everything was perfect—they sometimes bickered over silly things, like who had been supposed to feed Lucifer, or who had tracked mud onto the couch (usually it was Sparrow, but they preferred to blame each other, as Sparrow was too perfect in their eyes to ever make a mistake). Theodore really did have a temper, though he was careful not to let it come to real harm when it flared.

One of their biggest arguments centered around church. Mary hadn't gone since they married—at first she'd been too lovestruck to even think of it, and then the bad weather had held her off. But she missed going, even if she did understand that it wasn't going to church that made you a good person. She missed the community of it, and the singing, and the feeling that she was connected to an ancient tradition that spanned back to early humanity.

Theodore refused to go. "I've got better things to do than sit on a hard wooden bench and be lectured by my father," he'd say whenever she tried to sway him.

"But think how happy he'd be, if you went!" Mary would say, and Theodore would shrug maddeningly. Finally, they agreed to disagree, and Mary decided to go on her own, which was a good thing in the end anyway, because it gave her alone time to imagine and pretend—and to remember who she was as an individual person, outside of the coziness of her marriage.

Often, as she walked to church, she'd talk to Grandma, telling her stories out loud and filling her in on everything her life had become—pretending that the woods were Grandma's ears. Mary kept waiting for the missing to go away, but it didn't, though it did seem to become more and more bearable as time passed.

It helped that Theo missed Grandma, too. Sometimes, when they both especially missed her, they'd sweep—but not too well into the corners—and then they'd lay on the couch in silence together and admire the way the dust danced in the warm yellow sunlight. The dust had a way of tying you right into the moment, so that not even missing Grandma hurt so badly.

Even with the happiness of her new life, there was one thing that troubled Mary—she felt an irrational dread of her birthday as it drew nearer. It was the last ghost from the past that she hadn't been able to exorcise, and it haunted her. Sometimes at night she would have a nightmare in which the mayor knocked on the cabin door and told her that she'd stolen her life, and wasn't supposed to have it, and that she'd have to go to court. And then Alice would name her guilty, and they'd throw her in jail.

"I'd like to spend the morning of my birthday alone," Mary had announced at breakfast the day before.

Theodore looked up from his porridge, surprised. "Why's that?"

"I'm going to climb the mountain."

They both looked out the window, to where the mountain cast a purple shadow over the woods and lake. They still had yet to make it to the top together—it had been a cold spring, and on the top of the mountain, ice and snow dominated the landscape.

Theodore was wise enough not to caution her. All he said was, "Why not you bring Sparrow with you? She could use the romp. I'll have a good meal ready for you when you get home."

Mary spent the rest of the day with Theo's maps, routing her path to the top. She decided on a trail that would take her around the lake to where one of the meadows bloomed purple with lupines each spring, and then up one of the ridges to the top. She'd circle down on the other side of the lake, through the thickest part of the oak forest.

On the morning of, Theodore kitted out her new canvas pack with two tin water bottles, a satchel of nuts, and several other snacks. He also packed his warmest, felted sweater and his new fur-lined hat, so that if she grew cold on the top she would have something to wear, and let her take his favorite walking stick—a knobbly old thing with an indent on the thumb that made it particularly comfortable to hold.

Mary set out with the first rays of sun that spilled over the mountain, determined to make it to the top and back in record time. It seemed to her that if only she could get to the top, maybe she'd finally be able to stop worrying about her destiny. It didn't make sense exactly, but humans rarely do, and Mary was as human as anyone else.

On the way around the lake, she passed Simon's cottage. It was shuttered against the chill early morning, and she was surprised to see Simon sitting out on his porch, his fingers steepled in his lap, his gaze preoccupied as it rested on the lake.

Mary was grateful that he only lifted his hand in a wave— she was eager to be off, and didn't feel like explaining her mission this morning and seeing the pity on his face. She waved cheerily back and then disappeared into the woods again with a deep sense of relief.

Sparrow was a perfect walking partner—she was quiet and joyful, and she never left your sight for too long, so you didn't have to worry about where she might have gotten to. Mary enjoyed watching her white-tipped tail bob through the underbrush.

At moments she would pause, and the plume of it would be gorgeously illuminated in sunlight, and Mary would remember to notice all the other beautiful things in the world.

Her spirits lifted as she walked, until she was humming under her breath in rhythm with her steps. When she reached the meadow, she filled her pack with armfuls of decadent lupines to bring home to Theo, breathing in their scent and relishing the warmth of the spring sunshine on her face.

Then, with a square of her shoulders, she set off into the woods on the opposite side. She'd yet to explore them, and they beckoned welcomingly—crab apples lined the outer rim of the woods, and they bloomed with heady-smelling white flowers. Beyond them, ancient oaks darkened the skyline.

She walked into the oak stand with caution—the woods quickly became very twisted and dark. But Sparrow was beside her, bright and cheerful, and so she picked up the tune again and whistled as she walked, and reminded herself that there was nothing in the woods that wanted to hurt her.

It was a long walk to the base of the mountain, and with the first ascents her pulse started to pound in her wrists so heavily that she worried maybe she'd inherited Grandma's poor heart. But soon her whole body had warmed to the exercise, and she began to feel hardier as she walked.

By the time she reached the first view she'd forgotten to worry about her heart—or her destiny, or anything else for that matter—and simply enjoyed the shape of the landscape as it unfurled before her.

She knew she was nearing the real climb upwards when the trees began to shrink back from the sky, and the patches of blue in the canopy above became larger and larger. Soon even Sparrow had slowed her rambles, and stuck close to Mary's legs as they thrust their way against gravity, and up the side of the mountain.

It was a delight to watch the trees recede altogether, until they were low and scrubby on either side of her, and the whole of the land spread out before her like a tapestry to the northeast. Theodore had told her that when she got to the top she'd be able to see all the way around the mountain to the neighboring range to the south.

There were few signs of life this high, only the occasional crow winging its way above the trees below like a black shadow. Her thighs burned with the effort of climbing, and as the trail reached a pitch steeper than anything she'd faced yet, she had to stop frequently to catch her breath. Her blood thrummed in her head like a drum.

It was hard to tell where the top of the mountain was, and every once in a while she'd have to stop to examine the shapes around her and compare them to the map. Mostly she just tried to go up, and hoped for the best.

At one point she rounded a large boulder and found herself on an outcropping of granite. A scree of loose rock tumbled right up to its edge, and below there was a thirty-foot drop before the scrub rose up again from the ground. Mary backtracked, but the other routes were too steep to be managed. She would have to risk the precarious walk across the scree, or turn around.

Her stomach clenched with every step that she took, terrified that one wrong movement would set the loose rocks rolling. Behind her, Sparrow moved easily, picking her way over pebbles and boulders alike.

At last they reached the far side, and Mary clambered up onto solid earth gratefully. She had to sit for a moment so that her head could stop spinning. Even in that short pause, the wind whipped away her body heat, and she quickly became chilled. She pulled Theodore's sweater out of her pack and put it on, very glad that he had thought of it. It blocked most of the wind out, and now that she was a bit warmer, she didn't feel so afraid of the mountain.

Sparrow brushed against her leg and led the way up an almost vertical wall of solid granite. It was so steep that

Mary feared she would slide right off, but after a few steps she found that her boots gripped the rough texture of the rocks well, and it wasn't quite as steep as she had imagined it to be.

The rocks were patterned with lichen and moss in subtle hues of frosted green and violet. Mary tried to focus on those and imagine the patterns she might sew to capture their textures, instead of worrying about sliding off the mountain into thin air.

After one last scrabble upwards—she'd broken a sweat now that she was moving with the sweater on—Mary stopped and realized that there was no more up.

She turned in a circle—in every direction the ground dropped away from her boots, and to the south she could see unbroken trees and a river glinting in the late morning sunlight.

Sheer, wild pleasure burst through her body, and she lifted her arms into the chill wind, her heart still pumping from the exertion of getting there. She had the sudden urge to shout, to hear her voice slam and reverberate against distant surfaces, and so she bellowed into the wind.

If anyone from the village had seen her, they would've thought she was as uncouth and wild as her husband. But she was happy—fully and freely happy, one year from the day when she'd thought she would never be happy again.

After a good long shout, and a good long listen as her voice rolled back up to her from the sticks and the stones in the valley below, Mary sat down to eat her snacks and drink some water.

She was hesitant to go back down now that she had made it to the top, but the thought of the chicken pot pie Theodore was making at home roused her into action. She clambered down the sheer rock face and helped lift Sparrow down—up was apparently easier than down—and then picked her way back across the scree.

After that the going was easier, though her toes did hit the front of her boots until they were sore and throbbing. Slowly, the moss and lichen became scrub, and then scrub became forest thick with trees gnarled from the harsh winds.

The ground descended steadily, and eventually the underbrush lessened as she reached the tall oak forest. It was a pleasure to walk through after the brambly blueberry bushes that occupied the high places on the mountain. They didn't grab at her clothes, for one, and she was able to see through the giant trunks to a sea of ferns, which curled as elegantly as violin-heads.

She had just stopped to examine a particularly fat, whiskery curl of a fern when something white flashed through the trees. Automatically, Mary ducked, and then gasped as a small bird fluttered up in front of her face.

A bird! A small, white bird, with a scroll clenched in its beak. Her heart pounded in her chest, and she felt suddenly dizzy. It dropped its scroll meaningfully at her feet, and landed on a branch nearby to wait.

Mary picked up the scroll with trembling fingers. On the outside, in steady, slanting handwriting, someone had written,

My humble apologies for getting this to you so very late.

At that, she had to sit down. Thankfully, the ground was covered in thick moss. She pressed one palm into the welcome cushion of it, trying to steady herself.

She held a finger to the ribbon that held the scroll closed. But instead of tugging at the end of it to open it, she hesitated.

After a long moment, she held it up to the bird.

"Apology accepted," she said. "But it turns out that I don't need this after all."

It fluttered off the branch and gripped the paper gently in its beak, its little black eyes twinkling kindly at her. With a sudden thrust of its wings, it soared up through the trees and vanished into the white of the clouds.

Down below, Mary watched her destiny disappear—and smiled.

About the Author

Sarah Buckleitner is a science writer and author of Little Birds and Other Small Magic. Little Birds will be her first published novel, but it's far from the first in her library of tales. She's penned three other young adult novels on topics ranging from mermaid sci-fi to nightmares that come alive. Sarah is also the author of the blog, Feathery Thoughts, where she shares think-pieces on everything from parenting to grief. When not writing articles about climate change, novels, or blog posts, Sarah can be found watching her husband cook, or playing pirates in the treehouse out back with her two sons.

Coming Soon

from Sarah Buckleitner

The Dovecote: Small Magic Book 2

"The Dovecote," a forthcoming novel, unfolds in the enigmatic town of Tolling Bell, Maine, and serves as a concurrent narrative to the events in "Little Birds and Other Small Magic." This story centers around Simon, the second Primrose boy, whose life takes a pivotal turn just before the incident involving Mary's missing bird.

In Tolling Bell, each resident receives a visit from a little bird delivering a scroll on their eighteenth birthday, revealing their destiny. As Simon approaches his own significant birthday, the town is still reeling from his older brother, Theodore's, unexpected decision. Despite the town's assumptions and his father's hopes, Theodore doesn't follow the anticipated path of becoming the community pastor, even though his destiny scroll allowed for that possibility.

When Simon's eighteenth birthday arrives, all eyes are on the second son to see if his bird will be more direct in declaring the community's next pastor. As Simon contemplates the enormous responsibility of taking up his father's mantle, his bird arrives. Things don't go exactly as expected, and Simon finds himself dealing with more responsibility for the town than he ever imagined. The Dovecote provides a new lens on the events occurring alongside Mary's story, while also delving into unique challenges and revelations that Simon faces, altering his life and potentially the future of Tolling Bell itself.